KLITZMAN'S ISLE

A Novel of Bondage and Submission

I0659322

Paul Blades

Copyright © 2006 Paul Blades

Cover Photo@AlexMax/Canstockphoto.

978-1-937335-12-0ISBN-13

Dark Visions Publications
darkvisionspub@gmail.com

CHAPTER ONE

THE FRENCH GIRL

A beautiful, pale skinned, slender young woman is lying unconscious on a round, carpeted dais in the middle of a large, dimly lit room. A light shines directly above her, spotlighting her recumbent form. But for leather bracelets around her ankles and wrists and a steel collar around her throat, she is naked. She has long, shapely legs, delicate round hips. Her hair is long, straight and black. She is slumped over on her side, her legs scissored, the right over the left. A dark patch of hair peeks from between her thighs. The plush lips of her sex can just be seen through the abundant thatch.

Standing in a broad semi-circle around the young girl are three men. The man in the middle is a heavy set, well-muscled black man. He is tall, standing about 6'4". His hair is close cropped. His face is broad, thick lips, a large flat nose. He is wearing a reddish brown robe of light cotton with dark red piping. It wraps around his fit middle, tied by a yellow cord. The robe descends to just below his knees, which are bare, along with the rest of his legs and feet. The robe has short half sleeves, which flare out.

Standing on either side of him are two similarly outfitted men. The one on the right is Caucasian, perhaps Latino. His hair is brown, and is drawn into a short ponytail. His face sports several days of growth, probably designed to hide the four-inch long scar along his right cheek, as it partially does. He is not as tall as the man in the middle, standing about 5'11"

The man on the left is slender and tall, almost 6"2". His slightness of build hides a tightly compacted frame. The muscles on his arms are well toned. As he stands, his poise and natural grace are apparent. His hair is blond, cut almost to the scalp. He has no facial hair.

The men look admiringly on the supine form of the girl. Their visages bespeak a firm sense of purpose. A faint odor of burning coals fills the room.

As the girl begins to stir, the black man signals to the man on his right. Nodding, the Latino steps up to the dais. A slender chain descends from the ceiling. He quickly clasps the girl's wrists to the chain and steps away. The tall, blond man has stepped over to the wall and started a winch that will pull the chain upwards. He stops the machine just as the girl's hands rise slightly above her body.

A groan emanates from the shapely young prisoner. Her eyes blink open. She is still groggy and takes a few moments to absorb the strange scene. She is unsure whether what she is seeing is real or a terrible dream. Suddenly she realizes that what she is seeing and feeling is not a dream. She is naked, her wrists are chained. Three brooding, evil looking men are standing over her, watching.

There is a moment when the girl is so surprised at her surroundings that she stares blankly at the men. She moves to join her legs together and cover her breasts with her hands. Recovering from the initial shock, she speaks. She is speaking French. The men don't speak

French but the gist of what she is saying is not lost on them. Certainly she is expressing her fear and shock at her unexpected surroundings. Yesterday, she had been at a cocktail party. She had worn her black, strapless dress and matching high heels. She had been told that it would be an exclusive party. She knew no one there except the young Italian boy who had brought her. She had a drink. She felt dizzy. He led her to a bedroom. She had lain down. And now this.

The black man, obviously in charge, motions the tall man to raise the chain. The tall man restarts the winch, which begins to pull the girl's arms up over her head. Seeing her hands rising, the girl frantically tries to pull back on the chain. But the chain is strong and the winch that is winding it is sturdy, able to withstand the strongest paroxysms of fear and desperation that a young female can exert.

The rising chain forces the girl, first to her knees and then to her feet. She continues to fight its inexorable rise, but to no avail. She is speaking loudly, panic in her voice. Her eyes dart about the dimly lit room. The poor lighting hides its full contents from her. The spotlight that shines down on her further obscures her view. Dimly, in the background, she can vaguely make out a large, obesely fat man sitting in a brown leather armchair. He is smoking a cigar. His face is hidden.

The thin man rejoins the others when the still struggling girl has been pulled to her full height, her toes barely reaching the floor.

Two of the men step forward. The lithe, young woman tries to shy away from them. As they reach for

3

her ankles she tries to kick at them, to push them away. But the men are practiced and they easily imprison her ankles in their hands. Besides, with her body extended so, her toes just able to scrape along the carpeted surface of the dais, she is unable to obtain any purchase to add force to her flailing legs. The men quickly pull her ankles apart and affix them to chains on the sides of the dais. She is now fully suspended, her body forming an inverted 'y'. When they are done, the two men step back and observe the now helpless form of the frail, but well shaped, female before them.

The men now can more fully take in her splendorous features. Her face is long and narrow, with a delicate, slightly upturned nose. The lines of her jaw are graceful and her eyes, somewhat wide apart, are a luxurious green. The breasts, while small, stand out firmly from her body, topped by long, dark, thick nipples. Her belly is taut, her hips curvaceous. The muscles of the legs, which strain to fight their confinement, are thin, but well toned. The hairy bush at the center of the girl's legs does not hide the now wide open sex. Although young, barely 19, the girl has just slight baby fat around her waist. Someone has made an excellent choice.

The man in the middle, the heavy set black man, now moves forward to the girl, stepping up on the dais. He runs his hand down her naked hip, feeling the soft and supple skin. He stares into her eyes as he fondles her breasts with both hands. The girl has stopped her futile struggle and is silent. This man frightens her. He has the look of a brutal, ruthless man, one who would enjoy hurting her. But he must also have the answer to

4

why she is here, how she got here, what is to become of her. He does, but he says nothing to her.

The Latino steps up and hands the black man a tasseled whip. The girl sees it and, knowing that it is for her, renews her pleas. The words mean nothing to the black man. Although he cannot understand them he knows what is being said because he has heard it many times before in many languages. He rubs the whip tantalizingly along the girl's breasts, stomach and thighs.

Her words are now understandable since they are almost universal. "No! No! No!" she cries. She sees that she is about to be whipped. She does not know why, but she hopes that her pleas can dissuade this menacing madman from inflicting harm on her. But the man will not be deterred. He stands back, leaving ample room to swing the whip and exert the strength of his thickly muscled arm.

"Whack!" The whip strikes the girl across her stomach. It leaves angry red welts. The girl gasps. Before she has the chance to scream, another blow descends. This one strikes the inside of her right thigh. The strands of the whip reach almost fully around her leg, leaving a semicircular trail. She now has time to react and utters a high pitched squeal, almost a screech. A third blow strikes her breasts, which causes the girl to scream in pain.

The man is insensitive to her wailing complaints as he continues his pummeling of her flesh. He strikes the inner portion of the left thigh, the stomach and breasts again. He is moving around her as he swings the whip. The two other men are standing back, enjoying the spectacle. A blow to the girl's divide increases the pitch of her complaints dramatically. The man moves to her back and repeats his exertions there. The girl is crying now, her sobs interspersed with wails and screams as each blow falls.

Finally, the whipping is done. Her body is crisscrossed with the evidence of her suffering. The black man hands off the whip to the Latino and nods to the tall blonde man. He quietly steps over to the shadows and returns with a rod of iron. He holds it with heavy gloves. Its tip is a fiery red. It is a branding iron. The Latino returns and releases the ankles of the still sobbing girl. She does not see the branding iron behind her and has no idea what new cruelty is in store. She expects to be raped, and she will be shortly. But she cannot conceive of being branded. She does not know that she has become property. And property must be marked.

The Latino approaches the girl and presses his body against hers. His chest mashes her small breasts against her body. She can feel his stiff member beneath his robe, smell the man's sweat. But this is not yet part of the sexual assault that she is soon to experience. This is something else.

Locking his legs around the girl, the Latino holds her tight. She is immobilized; her ass juts out as the Latino presses his loins against hers. The tall man acts immediately as he sees the young woman secure and perfectly posed. With a sure hand, he pushes the red end of the rod against the girl's skin, near the top of the right buttock, towards the side near the hip. The girl stiffens and screams at the unanticipated, excruciating pain. The brand is held there for three seconds and then removed. It has left a deep gouge in the girl's flesh. She has fainted.

The black man takes a small dollop of ointment, tinged in red. He rubs it across the fiery wound. The ointment will disinfect and promote the healing of the blistered flesh. The dye will seep into the raw skin and color it. He steps back. The girl is limp in her chains, muttering some prayer or plea, lowly. The Latino joins the others behind her. As they pull off their robes, in preparation for this female's first sexual use as a slave, they pause to admire the tall man's handiwork. There, burned permanently and indelibly into the girl's flesh is a bright red, three inch high, cursive "*k*".

CHAPTER TWO

WE MEET HARRY

Let me introduce myself. My name is Harry Wiggins. I am a man of various talents, most of them illegal. I started out my adult life as a petty thief, car burglaries and the like, all free lance stuff. It wasn't long before I had graduated to second storey jobs and a few small holdups. After a short spell at Vacaville State Penitentiary, I was "adopted" by an operator called Tony Bianco. He had a little thing going in Atlantic City: gambling, a bit of prostitution, loan sharking and some of the other cottage industries of organized crime.

So I worked for Tony for a few years. The pay was good and the side benefits were terrific. I had a free pass at his local whorehouse and I got some trim there just about every day. And there were the showgirls. Well, they didn't work unless Tony said so. Usually he took the best of them, but even the girls in the second row were dishes. Being nice to me and the other boys was a precondition to working.

From time to time Tony would send a girl up to our clubhouse at the north end of town for a little weekend party. What they didn't know was that they would be the featured attraction at a gangbang. We saw lots of those girls later at the whorehouse. Sending them to us was Tony's way of breaking them in.

Every good thing has to come to an end. I got nabbed after doing this guy, an ex-fighter with soup for brains named Jimmy Tiger, who had screwed up a fix on a fight. He was supposed to get the local fighter to take a dive. He didn't and Tony sent me looking for him. Right after I put a bullet between his eyes, the Feds came storming in. How was I to know the guy was wired? Too bad the Feds weren't a little bit quicker. They would have saved me and Jimmy a lot of trouble.

Seven months later, Tony, me, and a few of the boys, were all standing before a Federal judge being sentenced on a racketeering beef. Tony got 25 years, the other boys got 10 years apiece. Because of the homicide, I got life.

Life in the Federal system meant life. I was not a happy camper. Tony told me he'd take care of me, but that lasted about fifteen minutes, since he was sent to a medium facility in Oklahoma and I was sent to Atlanta, a max. Boy, had I graduated.

I had done about thirty months of my life bid when a bull told me I had a visitor. I was working in the laundry and was very happy to escape the steaming heat for a while. As he led me from the laundry, I realized that we're not heading for the regular visiting rooms, but to an office in the Administration wing. I shuffled down the hall, a chain link belt around my wrists and shackles on my feet. When we reached the door to a small conference room, the guard opened the door and let me in.

There were two men in the room, both dressed in grey, shiny suits. The one was tall, with short blond hair, a heavy build, about 35 years old. The other was medium height and had scruffy brown hair. He was slender, his face was kind of pushed together, his nose sharp and pointy. He was a little older, pushing 45. They were both obviously cops. "Sit down, Harry," the tall one said. He motioned to the guard. "You can take the cuffs off, we can handle him."

The guard eyed the plainclothes dick sullenly. He didn't like being ordered around by pointy-toed Washington types. But he did what the guy said and left the room.

A pack of cigarettes and my old Zippo lighter were tossed on the table. "Have a smoke, Harry." The tall guy said. He seemed to be the spokesperson.

It was kind of a kick to see my old lighter again. I had lost it when I got arrested. I tooled up a smoke and fingered the lighter gently. My former life. These guys were smart. This was a good way to start off, getting me to think about the outside. Whatever they wanted, I figured that it might mean a ticket out of here.

"Thanks," I said nonchalantly.

"Harry, I'm Agent Bederson and this is Agent Mulattieri. We've come all the way from Washington to see you."

"I'm real honored," I said.

"Yeah, I suppose you would be, Harry. After all, you're doing a life stretch and haven't had a single visitor for almost three years. I guess Tony hasn't come through for you, has he?"

"Well, he's busy," I retorted. I took a deep drag off of the smoke. I was hoping they'd let me keep the pack.

"You might say so." The big guy walked around the table and put his foot on the side rung of my chair. His right hand was in his pants pocket and his other hand was on the table. He was almost leaning over me. "Did you know that he's at the minimum in Jarvis, Texas? Nah, you probably didn't. Last I heard he was even getting laid on Sundays. Seems he bought himself a hooker and had her marry him so that he could get conjugal visits. They say she's quite a number."

"That's good for Tony," I said. "He was always a lucky guy." My cigarette was almost finished and I looked around for someplace to put it out. I had been flicking the ashes into my hand. Last thing I wanted was some bull getting on my case for dirtying up his conference room.

The little guy pulled an old Sucrets tin out of his pocket and dropped it in front of me. I popped it open with one hand, tossed in the ashes and stubbed out the butt.

"You know," I said, "I'm really happy to get the news about Tony, but something tells me that that's not what you came here to talk to me about."

"Ah, Harry, they were right about you. You're smart. Real smart. And that was a neat shot when you put the Tiger away, right between the eyes. Like you'd been doing it all of your life."

"Yeah," was all I replied.

"Well Harry it just so happens that agent Mulattieri and I have come to make your day. We're going to make you an offer you can't refuse." Bederson chuckled at his Godfather reference, all too appropriate in my case.

"You see," he continued, "we need a guy like you. We need a guy with a certain cachet. A tough guy with some brains. And that's you Harry." Bederson stepped away from my chair and took a seat across from me.

"You ever hear of a guy named Klitzman, Harry?"

"Can't say that I have," I answered.

"Well let me say that if there were such a thing as a criminal mastermind, this guy Klitzman is it. He runs a criminal enterprise that is international in scope. He trades in just about every form of contraband you can think of and he's got a hold on some very highly placed people." Mulattieri had taken a seat at the table and was scrutinizing me intently.

"So what's this got to do with me," I asked, lighting another cigarette.

"You see Harry, your Uncle Sam is really interested in this guy Klitzman. Not too much is known about him, but we do know that he's been able to, let's say, 'influence' U.S. policy in rather strange ways. The State Department has called Klitzman's little island hideaway off the coast of Africa, forbidden territory. And there are certain activities that he engages in in this country and around the world that go pretty far beyond the pale."

"Okay, so," I interjected.

"So, we want you to become friends with Mr. Klitzman."

"How the fuck am I supposed to do that?" I asked incredulously.

"Have faith, Harry, we can arrange it."

"So the FBI's going to get me out of here, send me to Africa so I can buddy up with some guy who would probably smell a rat from about a hundred miles away. You gotta be nuts." I stubbed out my cigarette. "You're wasting my time." I started to get up to leave. Bederson put a hand on my shoulder.

"Harry, we're not from the FBI," he said.

"What?"

"We're not from the FBI," Bederson repeated.

I looked over at Mulattieri and he just shook his head.

"Right now I can't say who we work for, but let's just say we have a lot of juice. We can make things happen for you Harry. How'd you like to get back in the saddle, get outside, get back to work?"

"You want me to go out and commit crimes?" I was really flabbergasted now.

"If it's in the national interest Harry, we can justify almost anything."

"Okay, okay," I said, "let's suppose I agree to this. First of all, I'd be risking my neck every day. If this guy Klitzman is as big as you say, he'd have my skin up on his wall if he even had a suspicion that I was a rat. Second of all, I'd like to get out, yeah, but where is this all going to lead? How would I know that you have the juice to get me off any beefs I get into for this guy Klitzman? And how long would I have to do it?" I paused. "Jeeze, I'm talking like this thing could actually really happen."

"Harry, listen to me," Bederson said.

And he explained to me that Klitzman loved to recruit from Federal prisons, that he liked tough guys who were doing life bids. He had the juice to spring them on some fake pardon or something, and then he set them to work for him. The guys he picked tended to be very grateful and eager to do just about anything Klitzman asked. Bederson said that his people knew of this guy who was on the inside, who scouted for

13

Klitzman. Bederson wouldn't tell me who he was. But this guy had been looking at my records. Bederson's people believed that he was going to recruit me.

I gave the scenario that had been painted to me some thought. I had nothing to look forward to in the joint other than either someday getting a shiv in my ribs for some real or imagined slight to some other con, or breathing my last staring at the ceiling of the hospital ward after another thirty or forty years of excruciatingly repetitive days.

But if I took Bederson's offer, I could get out, breathe some real air, maybe put on some moves. If I got away with ratting out Klitzman, good. If I didn't and ended up as shark bait, well I would still have had some fun. And there was a third possibility, one that I was sure had occurred to by erstwhile benefactors. I could meet up with Klitzman and 'go native', that is, really become one of his boys. I might not last long, but I would be living on my feet and not on my knees.

As I saw it, there was really nothing to lose. I agreed.

Bederson told me that, when Klitzman's man contacted me, I was to alert him by sending a letter to this lawyer. They would work out a means for me to stay in contact. He also reminded me again that they were not the FBI and that they were not limited to purely lawful remedies. I caught his drift.

Two weeks went by when I was approached by one of the 'tough' guys from the white power gang at the prison. Prison life revolved around gangs and protection. I was kind of protected through my relationship to Bianco, but that was fading fast as time went on. To make a long story short, this guy thought it would be a good idea if I did a hit for his group. My benefit would be protection from the other gangs. They didn't want to have the hit done by someone already known as a member because they would immediately be identified as suspects.

The guy they wanted me to hit was well known as a snitch, so I had little qualms about doing the job. It was not getting caught that was the trick. Friday night was movie night and everyone would be in the mess hall. I knew that that was when this snitch would take a 'tour' of certain work areas that were well known as hiding places for contraband. I knew that he would be searching the kitchen area of the mess hall, and so I quietly slipped into the kitchen and waited. I was armed with a sharply honed knife made from a part from somebody's bed frame and covered with tape at the handle. As the snitch passed by, I jumped behind him, held his mouth closed, and drew my knife across his throat. In 15 seconds I was back in the mess hall watching the movie.

There was a big hubbub about the death of the snitch, but it all died down after a week or two. After a while, the tough guy let it be known that he wanted to talk to me. I met him in the prison yard. We walked out of hearing of the other cons. He congratulated me on my success and told me that he had another proposition for me.

"How'd ya like to get outta here," he said.

I knew what was coming but had to play dumb. "Fuck you," is all I said.

He insisted that he was on the level and explained

to me roughly what Bederson had told me. He left out his benefactor's name and where I would be going. All he stressed was that I would be out of the country, given a new identity and would be rolling in clover. I told him that if he could pull it off, I would jump at the chance.

Another two weeks went by and I was advised that I was being transferred to a medium joint near Huntsville, Alabama. I had sent the letter to the lawyer who was supposed to be my contact, but had received no word back. I packed my stuff, what little there was of it, said so long to my cellmate and followed the guard to the sally port. My stuff was checked; I was bedecked in chains and then led out to a waiting van.

It was a normal prison van, basically a minivan with reinforced windows, double locks and a heavy steel screen across the rear of the front compartment. Two green uniformed Federal prison guards were waiting for me. They loaded me up and we were on our way.

About five miles outside of Atlanta, the van suddenly veered off of the expressway, went about three miles down a small two lane road and then turned into a gravel driveway that snaked deep into the woods. We stopped in front of an old, apparently abandoned garage. The guard on the passenger side hopped out and opened the side door of the van. "Get out," he said in a gruff voice. It was the perfect place for a hit and I assumed that somehow this guy Klitzman had smelt a rat and was having me put in a hole. But when I got out, to my surprise, the guard freed my cuffs and ankle chains. The other guard threw me some civilian clothes and told me to change. I didn't know what was up, but

I didn't need to be told twice. I changed quickly. While I changed, the first guard drove the van up to the garage. He opened the double bay door and then drove the van in. On the other side of the van was a brand new looking, black Lincoln. He tore off his uniform and put on some clothes he found in the front seat. The other guy ran up and did the same from the passenger's side. I was stunned, and stood in the middle of the driveway in my new clothes ogling the two men. One yelled back at me.

"For Christ's sake, get in the fucking car!"

I ran over and got into the back seat. My prison garb was thrown into the van along with the guard uniforms. The Lincoln pulled out, the door was closed and we were out of there. It all took less than three minutes.

Three hours later, we pulled into the parking lot of a small commuter airport near Columbus. A small plane was waiting for me. I was hustled over and climbed in. In two minutes I was in the air.

The pilot didn't tell me to shut the fuck up, but he made it clear he had nothing to say. He handed me a bag that had a sandwich and a Coke in it, and just kept his eyes on the sky and clouds ahead of us.

It was almost dark when we flew into Miami International Airport. When the plane stopped, the pilot handed me a 9" x 12" brown envelope. In it was a slightly worn, black wallet, about $250 in cash and, a driver's license and passport, both with my picture on it, and both in the name of Robert Cox. There was also a plane ticket to Caracas, Venezuela. The pilot spoke to me.

"Now, don't fuck this up. Go into the terminal. Go to gate 12. Check in and wait. Don't go anywhere, don't do anything, don't talk to anyone, got it?"

"Sure," I said.

"You'll probably be watched. You'll be met in Caracas. Just do what you're told."

"Okay, okay," I said.

I got out of the plane and walked over to the terminal. The pilot had handed me a small suitcase, which, I supposed, contained some clothes and other travel stuff. I did what I was told. I stopped only to buy a paper and a cup of coffee. I was spooked when I saw the metal detector. I had no idea what was really in the suitcase. But I had gotten this far without a hitch and figured that Klitzman's boys would make sure that the bag and its contents would pass muster.

In fact, I sailed through the checkpoint. I walked down to gate 12, checked in and waited. My flight was in an hour.

About forty minutes later I boarded the plane and found my seat. Business class. There was some shitty film and crap food. I wiled my time away listening to jazz on the earphones. I must have nodded off because the next thing I knew the plane was landing. I breezed through customs. When I entered the airport proper, I saw a man holding a cardboard sign with the words "Mr. Cox" written on it. I walked up to him. "I'm Cox," I said.

"Please to come with me," was his only reply. He took me to a taxi and then drove me, again without a word being spoken, for about an hour. We stopped at yet another airport, a small one, with, again, a plane waiting for me. In a minute I was back in the air.

Now this guy was talkative. In fact I couldn't get him to shut up. He told me all about this tourist he fucked the night before, his car, how much he loved flying, how the weather sucked down here and on and on and on. When I asked him where we were going, he said only, "You'll see."

This flight was about another four hours. The only food the pilot had was a bag of peanuts. He let me have half.

I could see that we were flying mostly southeast over a long expanse of jungle. I thought to myself that it would be a rotten place to have to land, when suddenly the plane took a dive. For a moment I visualized myself as crocodile meat. But as I looked ahead, I saw a small clearing. Gabby circled the plane and prepared to descend.

CHAPTER THREE

THE FRENCH GIRL GETS FUCKED

The men release the hands of the softly moaning, barely conscious girl from the chain and drag her over to a wooden apparatus standing not far from the dais. It has four legs spread about four feet apart, and stands about waist high. The legs support a small padded platform about three feet square. There are two round cuts on one side. The limp girl is draped stomach down onto the platform. Her ankles and wrists are affixed to rings in the legs. Her breasts fit neatly into the two holes.

The placement of the girl leaves her head at waist level and her legs spread wide, exposing her secret places. The bulky black man, who answers to the name of Rukimo, waives a small, pungent smelling vial under the girl's nose. She shakes her head, seeking to avoid the piercing odor. Rukimo grabs her hair and forces her to inhale the sharp scent. When he is sure that she is fully awake, he withdraws it and releases the girl's hair.

The girl is startled by her changed confinements. She pulls futilely at the fixtures to her wrists and tries to kick her ankles free. The apparatus, constructed of a heavy wood, is stained a dark mahogany and is anchored to the floor. There are heavy scratch marks on the legs where the young woman's hands are affixed, the claw marks of other desperate young women anxious to avoid their fates. The poor woman's exertions barely make the apparatus sway.

The Latino man is gently stroking the girl's ass. His name is Luis Santana, but everybody calls him "Cholo". The girl tries to see who is touching her and twists her neck around. She sees Cholo smiling at her. He is naked, as are the other two men. All the girl can do is attempt to wriggle her hips to shed the unwanted caresses, but the effort is wasted. She turns her head forwards and sees Rukimo holding his thick, jet-black cock in his hand. She knows better than to beg. These men are going to fuck her and there is no way to stop or dissuade them. She can't help but emit a tiny whine as she grimaces and tries to withhold her tears.

Rukimo has in his other hand what appears to the girl to be a strange instrument. Her mostly chaste upbringing has not familiarized her with the idea of a ring gag. But she sees the round ring of rubberized plastic and the straps affixed to it and knows that, whatever it is, it is meant for her. Rukimo momentarily pauses in his caresses of his cock to grab the girl's cheeks. His massive hand presses hard, and the girl's mouth opens. He pushes the ring gag into her mouth. She needs to open wide to admit the large ring. Rukimo jams it in forcibly. The girl is crying and kicking as she resists. But Rukimo is an expert. He has applied many a ring gag into an unwilling mouth. He presses the girl's cheeks harder causing her to squeal in pain. Ultimately, she surrenders by stretching her lips widely apart and admitting the heinous instrument.

It is obvious to her what is going to happen. Rukimo is going to shove his thick, black cock into her

21

mouth. It has hardened now and Rukimo steps nearer. He says something to the other men that she does not understand, but they all laugh. The girl is determined not to give these brutal and callous men the satisfaction of seeing her fight and protest against their use of her mouth. She holds her head still, not struggling, as Rukimo holds her hair with one hand and, with the other, aims his steely rod at the nice, round hole.

But Rukimo wants to play first. He rubs his cock across her outstretched lips, against her cheeks. She is disgusted by his antics. She has closed her eyes to shut out what is happening, and Rukimo rubs his cock there too, pushing against her eyelids with its tip. Her body is taut with tension. She feels someone stroking her exposed sex. She cannot turn to see who it is.

It is the tall, thin man, who is called Thorndike. He uses no first name and no one has ever asked him what it is. The name Thorndike is probably fictional anyway. He has been stroking the lips to the girl's pussy, watching it slowly respond. The girl tries to clench her thighs, but that is impossible. A small glistening of moisture appears and Thorndike makes a joke. There is more laughter.

Rukimo has decided that the time has come to push his cock past the ring of hard rubber inside the girl's mouth. He feels her tongue retreating from this harsh invasion. The girl's face registers her displeasure and a small moan escapes her lips. Rukimo presses forward, seeking entrance to the girl's throat. As she realizes what is happening, the girl panics. Her airway is obstructed by the huge, hard tube of meat. Her eyes open. Rukimo is staring down at her, amused. He is gently rubbing his cock back and forth across the opening to the girl's throat, just enough into it to prevent the passage of air.

The girl now is coughing and sputtering. Despite her earlier resolution to remain passive in the face of the invasions of her body to come, she is now jerking her body frantically, trying to twist and turn her head to expel Rukimo's member. From her throat comes plaintive wails.

Ultimately, the point comes where the girl is afraid she will die from lack of oxygen. Her head becomes woozy and her eyelids flutter. But Rukimo is experienced in these things and pulls his cock back just enough to permit the flow of air. The girl breathes in deeply, or as deeply as she can with Rukimo's cock in her mouth. Rukimo now presses forward again.

Having experienced the sensation of Rukimo's big, black cock down her throat once, the girl is ill disposed to receive it again. But the choice is not hers. This time, Rukimo glides his piece in slowly, relishing the widening eyes of the helpless female. He presses firmly on the back of her mouth, seeking entry to her throat. With a little pressure, it slides in, the bulging head blocking the entire passageway.

The helpless girl is gagging and choking. Her body convulses with panic. She believes that she will die, that she will be choked to death by a cock. The girl has not eaten or drunk for many hours. Otherwise, the heaving of her stomach could lead to disastrous results. Even so, the bile from her digestive tract leaps up and coats her esophagus, irritating the tender membranes.

Rukimo pulls out once more. He allows the girl to

choke and moan. Tears are flowing down her face. She tries to speak, to beg the black man to cease his torture of her. But that is not in the black man's mind. He needs to discharge his seed first and he intends to discharge it down her throat.

Four more times the girl is forced to swallow Rukimo's hard tube of meat. Each time, she chokes and coughs and whines and gurgles. Finally, Rukimo gives in to the pleasure of the constricting muscles around his cock. His eyes roll back as his cock throbs and jerks within the girl's throat. She can feel the convulsions of the flesh within, feel the warm jet of his spunk. As Rukimo pulls his now softening cock from her mouth he pats her on the cheek. "Good girl," he says, smiling.

It is now Thorndike's turn. He has been fondling the lips of the girl's vagina all along and she is unwillingly wet. He gives his cock a few tugs to stiffen it and presses it between her legs. The girl is no virgin, but she is young and her pussy is tight and hot. She had barely recovered from her ordeal at Rukimo's hands when she feels the lips of her crevasse being spread open and the unmistakable pressure of a prick in her tight sheath.

Logically, she should be resigned to being fucked. After all, she has just experienced a most savage use of her mouth. But logic is rare when desperate times are at hand.

Although she can form no words, the girl wails loudly. Only two boys had had her there. One she loved and the other loved her. Their use of her had been tender, sweet. Her whole body had tingled with pleasure as she was entered, that is, after the initial tearing of her virginal wall.

But now she is being entered by a hostile cock. She can't even tell which of the men it is. She tries to rock herself free, strains mightily to close her legs. It is useless. The device has been well tested.

Thorndike pushes himself into the girl all the way to the hilt. He sighs with enjoyment as its warm moisture and tender pressure causes his cock to transmit signals of pleasure to his brain. He has his hands on the girl's slender hips as he rocks back and forth. The girl's moans have subsided now as she has surrendered to the inevitable. But as Thorndike's hot tool agitates her nub of pleasure and caresses the tender walls of her vagina, she feels something that she wishes to deny. Her loins are starting to burn with passion. Her rocking and jerking on the wooden platform has begun to excite her.

Thorndike senses this shift in the girl. His hands now rub her fleshy rear orbs and the outside of her thighs. Leaning into her, he is able to reach around and grab her breasts, cupping and squeezing them. The girl feels this and, unwillingly, abandons herself to the rising urges inside her. She knows that she will soon come and she hates herself for it. Yet, she cannot ignore the pressure on the apex to her sex, the piercing of her loins by Thorndike's flesh, the rubbing on her nipples. She makes a futile effort to hold back her climax. Then the orgasm is upon her, her whole body shudders, she is moaning loudly through the gag. Her hands are tightly clenched and her toes curl.

It is the moment that Thorndike has been waiting for. He explodes as she does, calling out loudly words that she cannot understand. When his ejaculation is finished, he sighs deeply and presses his chest against the girl's back. Her sex is still twitching with small waves of pleasure and he can feel its contractions as they slowly subside.

Cholo is anxious for his turn. There is one more hole to explore. The girl feels Cholo's hands on the cheeks of her ass. She is exhausted and it slowly registers on her that another assault is about to begin. She is too forlorn and abject to protest. But her face perks up when she feels Cholo's finger trace the outlines of her pursed rear hole. The men are watching her face and laugh when it dawns on the girl that she is to suffer what she has only read about in books. Cholo has leaned around the girl to see her expression as he pushes his finger slowly inside. She can see him as she is able to turn her head slightly. He smiles at her. He says something in Spanish that sounds soothing, friendly. But the pressure of his finger on her anus belies the tone of his voice.

The girl begins to sob softly. She makes no effort to avoid the inevitable. Her eyes are crammed shut, her body limp. Cholo penetrates her ass to his knuckle and then inserts another finger. The feeling has gone from a strange and annoying sensation to a modicum of discomfort. Cholo stretches his fingers wide, preparing the entrance for the insertion of a thicker object.

The fact that the girl has let herself go limp, has surrendered to the inevitable, lessens the resistance to the entry of Cholo's third finger. The sensation of Cholo's fingers in her ass is mildly stimulating. A strange tingle flows from the tender tissue of her anus to her vagina. Maybe if she just relaxes and lets him have his way, the girl thinks, this will not be so bad.

But what she does not know is that Cholo's tool is the thickest and widest of the three. And the flexible width of three fingers does not approximate what she will soon feel.

Cholo speaks to Rukimo. It is a question. Rukimo assents and Cholo grins. He withdraws his fingers from the still virgin portal and retrieves the whip that had been used on the girl a short while before. She cannot see it and is not prepared for the slash of the whip against her upturned buttocks. It is as if a trail of fire has been lit across her skin. The girl shrieks with pain. Cholo wants to rape this girl, not fuck her. He wants her screaming and begging, not supine and abject. Again he strikes her haunches with the whip. The girl's cries emerge from her gag, rounded and deep, almost like the mooing of a cow. Thorndike points this out to the others and they laugh again.

Three more times Cholo strikes the poor girl's behind. The whip is many tasseled and so the pain is spread across her now reddened rear cheeks. She is still screaming when Cholo presents his cock to her smallest opening. Now she is protesting, her cries of "no, no, no," are distorted by the ring of leather in her mouth and emerge sounding more like "oh, oh, oh!"

Cholo wastes no time in pressing hard into the girl's bowels. He is tearing her delicate skin, but that's okay. She will have to get used to ass fucking anyway and the rear hole will have to be widened. The Hispanic continues to rock back and forth in the girl's ass while she continues with her frantic complaints. He is

27

building to a crescendo as his thighs tighten and his eyes close. He cries out some words in Spanish as he pumps his sperm deep into the girl's bowels. He withdraws only when he has felt his cock diminish to its ordinary size.

CHAPTER FOUR

HARRY MEETS TWO LADIES

The pilot descended quickly to the tiny field. As we got closer, I could see that it was not quite as tiny as it first seemed. The plane easily rolled to a stop, well within the limits of the hard baked, clay runway. After the plane landed, I was hustled off by the pilot.

"Got to make it back to civilization," he said.

I was left standing by the dirt runway by myself, my little suitcase at my feet. I watched the plane disappear over the treetops with some dismay. Where I was and what I was supposed to do here was totally beyond me. The landing strip was surrounded by jungle. A small road led off to the south. There was a small hut in the middle. After waiting a requisite time, and seeing no one else around, I walked over to the hut. The weather was sweltering and by the time I had walked the several hundred yards, I was drenched with sweat.

The hut was locked. It had no windows. I tossed my bag aside, frustrated. "What the fuck is going on?" I thought. First I had been hustled thousands of miles from the U.S. and then nothing. I didn't expect a welcoming committee and a band, but I did expect someone to at least meet me. I had no idea where I was, how I was going to get food or, more importantly, water, and where I was going to sleep.

Darkness fell swiftly. I was weighing the thought of

taking a chance and walking down the dirt road to see what I could find when I saw what could only be the headlights of a car coming up in the distance. I heard the rumble of an overtaxed engine. Then I saw it, a battered, old style jeep rumbling and tumbling over the rough dirt road. There was only the driver in the jeep and I hoped that it was meant for me.

The jeep pulled up to the hut with a roar and screeched to a halt. The driver was a small, dark haired kid, no more than 14. He was smiling at me and he spat out words that were incomprehensible. I got the gist though; he was telling me to get in. Having seen his driving skills first hand, I hesitated at first to hazard life and limb with him at the wheel. "Americano, Americano," he yelled gleefully. "Come een, come een!"

I had no other choice. Well, I did have one. I could have tossed this kid out of the jeep and driven the thing myself. But, it was dark, I didn't know where I was going, and someone, probably with a little weight around here, would miss the kid.

And so I climbed aboard with my little bag and off we went. It was a twenty minute journey of hair-raising proportions. As we bounced and swerved along the road, the kid was having the time of his life. I held onto the crash bar that someone had considerately affixed to the top of the vehicle. I had my bag tight between my knees.

We finally reached a small village. There did not seem to be any electric lights as candlelight flickered through the windows of some of the huts. There was a large wooden house at the end of the street, torches burning in holders affixed to the columns of the porch.

It was here that the kid pulled up. "Go een, Go een," he said. I stumbled out of the Jeep and the kid rapidly sped away, kicking up dirt and stones as he spun the tires. I hopped out of the way of the effluvia from the Jeep's wheels and stepped up onto the porch. It was broad and wide, running the length of the house. There were bags of some vegetative product strewn about, benches and a dilapidated easy chair. A dim light could be seen through a screen door. I knocked.

A loud scratchy voice called something hostile in Spanish or Portuguese. I didn't know the difference. I yelled back, stupidly, "Hello!"

I heard a low muttering and then heavy footsteps as from booted feet. A swarthy, black haired man appeared at the door. He was dressed in a brown and red floral patterned shirt that was open to reveal a taut, hairy chest and a flat stomach. He wore a dark beard along his chin and a thick, black mustache. He was slender, but carried himself in a way that you would want him to be on your side in a tussle. He wore faded jeans and, as I had surmised, cowboy boots.

"Oh," he said, "the Norte Americano. The boy pick you up, yes?"

"Yes," I replied, exasperated. "The boy pick me up."

"Come in, come in."

I opened the screen door and stepped into the dimly lit room. It was a small foyer, lit only by the reflected light of the room beyond. The man led me into this room. I was startled by what I saw.

Lying on the floor, her hands tied behind and hogtied to her ankles was a young, brown haired woman. I could tell that she was not a native by her pale complexion and the American style clothing. She had a cotton knit polo shirt on top and a pair of khaki shorts. On her feet were a pair of Reebocks and frilly white socks. She looked up at me forlornly as I entered. Her mouth was pulled into a tight grimace by a red bandana that had been tied around her head. She looked very unhappy.

As my eyes adjusted to the light, I saw another woman, her hands tied to a rope that was thrown over one of the rafters. She was also gagged. She also had brown hair, but hers was much longer, reaching down to the middle of her body. Her flowery cotton blouse was unbuttoned and her bra had been pulled beneath her breasts. Her shorts were around her ankles. Her pussy was still covered by the white vee of a pair of thong panties. She looked at me too.

The contents of two backpacks lay scattered around the room. Two cameras, two wallets and two passports lay in one pile. A tangle of women's clothing was jumbled into semblances of piles. There were some books, two canteens and two cell phones.

The thin Hispanic man nodded at the two forlorn girls. "They were snooping around. Now they will snoop no more." The man chuckled sneeringly.

"My name is Morianos," he said. "You are the guy for the plane tomorrow. Come in and have a seat." He shouted something loudly in what sounded like Spanish ending in the words "*dos cervesos!*"

A small, heavy set, gray haired woman came running in with two bottles of tepid local beer. Morianos grabbed one and nodded towards me to the peasant woman. She slid over to me and handed me the other beer. It was only slightly cooler than the tropical heat.

Morianos must have known what I was thinking. "Generator's out. Fix tomorrow. Tonight we use lamps."

There were two oil lanterns on small tables in the room. The flickering, pale yellow light they threw off gave the room a movie set quality.

"What are you doing," I asked Morianos as I sat down in a rattan rocking chair.

"Looking for stuff, what else," he replied. He dangled a gold plated watch in the air. "Rolex," he said with a grin. A gold tooth glistened from his mouth. Two other teeth seemed to be missing.

"Not much cash," he commented. "These fucking cunts were carrying traveler's checks."

"How disappointing," I replied.

"Yeah, it pisses me the fuck off. Where the fuck did they expect to cash traveler's checks around here? *Gringas estúpidas!*"

I sipped at the lukewarm beer. My stomach growled. "Is there any food?" I asked.

Morianos yelled out in Spanish again. About thirty seconds later the woman returned, this time with a bowl of steaming chili and a swath of bread. I knew that it was probably as spicy as hell, but I was famished, and I did have the beer.

With the combination of the bread and the beer, I was able to eat about half of the bowlful. Morianos had given up searching through the contents of the backpacks and stood up from the floor.

"Amigo, help me with this one. The other one

almost broke my back."

I wasn't sure what he meant. He stepped away for a moment and came back with a rope, one end of which he flung over the rafter.

"Come on, buddy, we've got to string her up." He pointed to the woman on the floor.

"What the fuck for?" I asked.

"To search her, man. You know, strip her."

The girl on the floor attempted to make a remonstrance at this idea. Her voice came out as a garbled whine. I looked at her pleading eyes. Well, I thought, if stripping was the worst thing that happened to her, she would be lucky.

"Okay," I said. "Let's do it."

Morianos stepped over and released the girl's ankles from her wrists. He looked over to me and smiled. "This is the tricky part," he said.

He pulled a thick hunting knife, about 8 or 10 inches long from a scabbard at his waist. He spoke to the girl. "If you give me any trouble, I cut you up with this. Understand, you piece of shit?" His voice was menacing. I certainly didn't doubt his words. I was sure the forlorn girl didn't either.

Morianos motioned to me. "Help me get her up."

We each grabbed an arm and lifted the girl to her feet. Once she was in a standing position, Morianos said to me, "Untie the bitch's hands and tie them in front. Do it good!"

I complied with Morianos' instructions. The girl's wrists had been tied tightly. That and the added pressure of the hogtie had left harsh red marks. She was whimpering as I retied her hands in front of her. I was a novice where tying women up was concerned, but I figured I could handle this.

Once her wrists were tied to each other, Morianos put his hunting blade away and stepped over to the girl with the end of the rope that hung from the rafter. He pulled her arms up swiftly, causing the girl to cry in surprise. Once she was dangling on her toes, he crossed the other end between her ankles and tied it off. The girl's own weight was keeping her hands aloft.

The sneakers came off first, then the dainty socks. Nothing there. Stripping the other girl was a little bit easier because of her blouse. But this one wore a polo shirt. Morianos pushed it up past her breasts, but it kept falling down. The girl wore a lacey white bra that covered small, but firm tits. I could see the tops, almost to the nipples, pushed up over the upper edge of the bra.

Morianos swore and pulled out his knife. Without further ado, he sliced the shirt from the neck down. At this impetuous act, the girl stiffened in fright. A small line of blood appeared at her stomach. Morianos took no notice. Putting the knife away, he pushed the bra up over the girl's tits. Now all was revealed. Her short, pert, nipples were hard with fear. A pale areola surrounded each of them. Her eyes were clenched shut and her whimpering increased.

Morianos, having satisfied himself that the girl hid nothing in her bra, took notice of the whimpering. He grabbed a nipple and squeezed hard. "Shut the fuck up!" he yelled.

The girl's eyes lit up. She cringed woefully. Her whining subsided, replaced with a mere sniffling. I tossed back the rest of my beer.

"Any chance of a refill?" I asked Morianos.

He yelled in Spanish to the back room and two more *cervesos* came out. He took a swig and peered into the eyes of the captive girl. "Any little surprises in your pants, *gringa*? Anything besides your precious pussy?"

Sweat was dripping down the face of the girl, more than could be accounted for by the heat. Maybe Morianos was on to something.

He unbuckled her shorts slowly, his eyes on the girl's face. She stared back, as if mesmerized. The room was silent except for the sound of a zipper being lowered. Lacey white panties appeared. Suddenly Morianos gave a shout of glee. "I knew it! I knew there had to be something!" He stepped back to show me.

There was a thin pouch taped to the inside of the right pocket of the young woman's shorts. Morianos tore it off and, checking the left pocket, pulled another packet free. He then pulled the shorts down to the woman's ankles. Quickly, he opened the first package. Several sheaths of dark green paper emerged. They were 100 dollar bills, at least ten of them. Morianos stuffed them into his pocket. The he tore opened the other. Another four or five hundred-dollar bills emerged, along with a small, embossed card.

Why would a young girl, ostensively a tourist, carry an official looking card secreted in her shorts? This was obviously the source of the woman's fear. Morianos gave a hoot when he read it. He showed it to me. It was an official press pass issued by the Republic of Venezuela. "So that's where we are," I thought.

Morianos spit in the girl's face. "A *journalista!*" he cried. He spat again.

He pulled his blade from his hip. "I should cut you up, you fucking whore!" he yelled. He brandished it in her face. He ran some words at her in Spanish. The only word I caught was "*puta*".

Now he commenced cutting the remnants of the girl's shirt from her body along with the bra. She struggled and whimpered as every last shred of clothing was stripped from her. She was curvaceous and a delight to see, especially for someone who had been locked up for as long as me. I stood there watching the show. When he was done stripping the girl, Morianos commenced slapping her tits repeatedly. The helpless woman let out little squeals of pain every time he struck her. All the time he kept yelling at her in Spanish. The girl swayed on her rope at the force of each blow. Morianos timed the blows perfectly so that her breasts felt the full force of his hands. I had never seen a girl's breasts slapped around like that and I was mesmerized as they rocked to and fro.

I did nothing to mollify Morianos' outburst. This was not my game. I was as much at Morianos' mercy as these two young captives. I had bigger fish to fry.

Finally, Morianos tired of slapping the weeping girl's breasts. They were pink and raw from their ordeal. The girl kept whimpering as she tried to halt her swaying body by jamming her toes into the floor.

Morianos grabbed his beer and took a long pull at the bottle. He removed the money he had taken from the girl from his pockets and slowly counted it. "$1,500," he noted. "Okay, now that's something." He stuffed the money back into his pants. "And tomorrow, you and your girl friend here are going to take a little trip. But tonight, I'm going to fuck the shit out of you." He was pointing his knife at the reporter.

Morianos turned to me pointing at the other girl. "You can have her."

Now I had been locked up for a little under four years: seven months awaiting trial, three years at Atlanta. I thought that I would never feel the soft squeeze of a pussy as long as I lived. The girl was attractive, nice sized tits, wide sensuous hips. But rape? I had never done that before, well, not actual forcible rape. The girls at Tony's clubhouse, they were sort of convinced into it. They were paid afterwards too. Not that I was a purist mind you. But an actual forceful rape? That was something else.

The Latino must have sensed my reservations. "What's the matter, man, you don't like pussy?" He laughed, "Don't worry, she'll never tell nobody, not where she's going. And by this time next week, she'll have had a hundred cocks up her twat."

I looked over at Morianos inquisitively.

He looked at me surprised. "You really don't know, do you?"

"Know what?" I answered.

"Know where you're going man!"

"Actually, I don't"

"You're goin' to Kliztman's place, man! Pussy galore!"

"And so?" I asked.

"So none of them girls are volunteers, you know what I mean? They're like sex slaves, man. Do anything you tell them."

The words of Bederson came back to me. He had said that Klitzman was into "every form of contraband you could think of". Why was he so deliberately vague? If I had known that Kliztman was a flesh peddler, I might not have taken the bait. Kidnapping and raping women were not my thing. But I guessed they were now. Here I was, hopefully on the last leg of my journey to Klitzman's island fortress, stuck out in the middle of the jungle with this fugitive from a "B" movie. There was no way to back out. Even if I could get back to civilization, what would I do? I had $250 in my pocket, not enough for a plane fare to Miami. All my connections were still in the joint and, most importantly, my protection. I looked at the comely, but forlorn girl. Do I fuck her or not?

Then I remembered another thing I had been told, both by Bederson and by the guys who had lifted me from Atlanta. The gist of it was, "Do what you're told." Nobody had told me to fuck this broad. I doubted that Morianos' say had any weight. If these girls were headed to Klitzman's island, they were, or would be shortly, his property. Maybe he wouldn't want me fucking around with his property? I had waited almost four years; I could wait another day, if what Morianos said was true.

So I decided, very reluctantly, to hold myself in check. That didn't mean that I couldn't relieve myself though. The girl was staring at me quite forlornly. She was probably contemplating her upcoming ravishment. I didn't need to dispel that notion immediately and so I let her enjoy the prospect a little longer. I stepped towards her and ran my hands over her breasts. They were warm and wet with the sweat of the girl's fear. She whimpered slightly as I caressed them, enjoying their heft, their softness and smoothness. I flicked the nipples with my thumbs, encouraging them to hardness. The girl's breasts fit nicely in my hands, just the right size. My cock was hard as a rock and I worried that I might shoot my load right in my pants.

I took a moment to calm myself and then slipped my lips over the girl's taut and neat left nipple. I almost swooned. Four years! It was a long time not to have been able to suck on a tit. I grabbed the girl's ass with my hands and pulled her body into mine. As I did, I increased the pressure on her hands from the rope above and she gave a little squeal of pain. I ignored her complaint and moved my lips to her other breast. I knew that I could not hold on much longer.

Leaning back, I pulled the girl's panties to her knees. Her bush was wiry and tangled. Her cunt lips were hidden, confined by the creamy thighs that were held together so closely. I didn't think I could hold myself in check if I explored any further and so I stepped back. I pulled my zipper down and freed my hard little boy. It was anything but little now and I encircled it with my right hand. The girl's eyes, wide as saucers, were fixated on my rampant cock. She looked as if she expected a show and so I gave her one. It took about three tugs and my Johnson exploded. I was close enough to her that three pulsing streams of cum landed on her stomach. My cock throbbed with pleasure. I could barely stand as my knees weakened with my climax. I let the sticky flow cover my hand as I encouraged my joint to greater exertion. Finally, it had had enough, and I slowed my efforts to a tender caress. "Good boy," I thought.

The hanging girl looked disgusted and surprised at the same time. I wiped my hand on her breasts. "Sorry honey, that's all I can give you tonight, I told her. "Maybe soon we'll get to know each other better."

I zipped my fly, careful to avoid nipping my small friend and then downed the rest of my tepid beer. Morianos had said nothing about where I was to sleep and I didn't want to go exploring, so I decided I would camp out on his couch.

First I went outside and took a long, gratifying piss over the edge of the porch. The dull flavored *cervesas* had gone right through me. I shook the last drops free and returned inside. I looked at the girl. She was quite a display. It had been a long time since I had seen a naked pair of tits, and these were just about world class. I didn't know whether I should let her hang or untie her so she could spend the night in some form of comfort. "Nah," I thought. Why take any risks with her? She was apparently in for far worse and I didn't want to be responsible for her escaping.

I stood and admired her pleasing form. As I did, I could hear a whining female cry from the next room. My girlfriend heard it too, her eyes darting about. She looked at me pleadingly. She tried to talk, obviously to plea for release. Well, no dice, not tonight. I would be up to my eyeballs in shit if I did anything like that. I just patted her cheek and told her good night. Then, after dimming the lanterns, I lowered myself to the couch. For a while, the moans and cries of a helpless female kept me awake. Morianos at play. But then the wails and shrieks subsided and all that was left was the soft moans of the brown haired beauty next to me, swinging at the end of a rope. I dozed off.

CHAPTER FIVE

HER ORDEAL CONTINUES

The three men take a respite from the torment of the young French girl. They don their robes and drift over to a small bar where they pour themselves some drinks. There is laughter and the exchange of ribaldries among them.

The girl hangs limply in her bonds. She has no choice, really, being affixed so securely. She tries to imagine what is going to happen to her. She cannot let go of the idea that there is some mistake, or that somehow she will be freed once the men are done with her. Her rear cheeks still burn from the combination of the whip and the forced invasion of her most private place. She can still taste in her mouth the residue of Rukimo's discharge. She is ashamed that she orgasmed when she was fucked by the thin man and closes her eyes and grimaces at the thought. She cannot close her mouth because it is still filled by the ring gag installed by Rukimo.

The men return to admire the girl's well-toned and curvaceous form. Rukimo reminds the men that they have yet to abuse her breasts. They agree that that must be done.

The female's bonds are loosened and she is drawn down off of the apparatus. She is grateful at being untied, but her feeling of relief is short lived. Once she reaches her feet, she is spun around and her arms are stretched backwards over the top of the device. Her wrists are affixed to the straps there on either side. A simple pumping mechanism, operated by foot, cranks the apparatus higher and higher until it presses up against her underarms and lifts her up. She is now dangling with her weight borne by her shoulders. Her toes barely touch the floor. As her arms are stretched back behind her, her breasts jut out like twin offerings.

Rukimo takes from the wall, where it and a variety of other instruments of torture are displayed, a 30" long bamboo cane, wrapped in leather. He bends it to ensure its suppleness and swings it quickly in front of him, creating a "whooshing" sound. Thorndike and Cholo stand on either side of Rukimo, glasses in hand, poised to enjoy the upcoming spectacle. As Rukimo raises his hand to strike, there is a command issued by the fat man who has sat in the darkness all of this time observing the abuse of the girl.

Nodding his assent, Rukimo removes the girl's gag. It seems that the fat man wants to hear her scream. Thorndike has another suggestion and Rukimo nods. Thorndike takes two long leather thongs from a cabinet and brings them over to where the girl is affixed. She knows she is to be beaten again and her eyes are watering in anticipation of the pain she is to suffer. Thorndike has a plan that will make the pain more sublime.

He approaches the girl, who tries to shy away from him. Her lips are moving and a tiny whisper for mercy escapes. Thorndike looks at her and smiles. He has tied one of the straps into a loop and he circles the girl's left breast with it. Drawing at the thong's loose end, he draws it closed until the breast is captured in a tight ring. He confines the other breast similarly. Then he runs the loose ends of the straps over the girl's shoulders and ties them off behind her neck. The tension of the straps pulls the breasts up, a more delectable target for the whip.

The men wait and watch as the breasts begin to swell under their confinement. They are turning a light shade of purple as unrefreshed blood becomes pooled there. The breasts are now like little purple balls extruding from the young girl's chest.

Thorndike amuses himself by pinching and pulling at the nipples and softly slapping the breasts so that they swing side to side. Realizing the pain that will accrue from the whipping of her swollen tits, the girl now begins to plead again for mercy. Her resolve not to beg has dissolved. For the men, this is a good start. She will be screaming and begging for mercy in greater earnest in one moment.

Rukimo lifts the cane again. This time no command issues for him to halt or delay, and he strikes the girl's left breast with the supple cane. The sound that the cane makes as it strikes her flesh is akin to a 'whump!' as the breast absorbs the blow. It is followed by a screeching yell from the girl. Rukimo delays, waiting for the pain of the first blow to subside before striking again. This time it is the right breast that is struck. The girl has never really stopped crying, but the volume of her sobs and wails had tapered off during the brief pause. Now they rise in a crescendo again.

The girl's whole body reacts to the blow. Her head

turns side to side as she screams in pain. Her legs contract and she places her feet on the sides of the frame pushing as if she could propel herself off of the device to which she is cruelly strapped. Her chest heaves as she draws in the breath to scream her protests and her pain.

Rukimo waits again. This time the girl knows that the pause is a deception. Another blow will soon follow. There is no reason to cease her loud pleas for a desistance in her torture.

She is telling the men that she will do whatever they want. She offers to suck their dicks, fuck them. She knows someone with money; she can get it for them. She protests her innocence of any wrongful deed. Finally, she invokes the name of her deity. It is all absolutely useless. None of the men have understood a word.

Rukimo has decided that he will speed things up a bit. He strikes a third blow, which is rapidly followed by a fourth and a fifth. The girl's agonized contortions threaten to injure her, as she twists and turns her torso to the detriment of her shoulders and arms. Rukimo decides that she has had enough for now. She will remember this day as long as she lives. It is her introduction into her new life. She has been given fine examples of the body's ability to absorb punishment.

The men are randy again, having watched the delightful performance of the young girl. It is agreed that they will all fuck her again. It is a simple matter to raise the girl's ankles and affix them to the top of the frame. She is now doubled up, her ankles by her ears. Her pussy is splayed open at just the right height.

Cholo claims first rights, as he was the last to enjoy the girl's body previously. All agree that this is appropriate and so Cholo sets himself in front of the girl, his cock poised at the entrance to her pussy. She opens her eyes to see the grinning face of the Latino. He has a gold tooth that gleams in the light. The girl has absorbed so much punishment that she has no strength to protest this new invasion of her body. As Cholo pushes himself deep inside her, she gives a little moan. Cholo is an expert cocksman and is not satisfied at the passive acceptance of his cock by the girl. And so he slowly ploughs the girl's deep shaft, making sure that his cock rides gently over the apex of her sexual organ. It takes a while, but the blood begins to stir in the girl. She doesn't want it, but nature must take its course.

When Cholo sees that she has begun to breathe heavily, he redoubles his efforts. He holds her head with his hand and jams his tongue into her mouth. She tries to twist away, to close her mouth, but Cholo has gripped her cheeks with his strong right hand and he forces her still. The girl is issuing little whining noises as she tries to fight back the surging lust in her loins. Ultimately, she can hold back no more and she begins to come, jerking her torso wildly. Cholo comes too, slamming his cock home repeatedly, as if to force out his discharge.

Thorndike supplants Cholo immediately. He wants to keep the girl on the boil. His long, thick cock slides in easily. The girl gasps at the new invasion and she is soon pumping her hips in a passionate frenzy. She comes twice more before Thorndike does.

Rukimo steps up for his turn. He holds his hard

cock in his hand and waits for the girl to calm herself. When she looks up, she sees his broad, jet-black face staring at her. Rukimo takes his hand and rubs the girl's pussy, capturing some of the combined discharges of the girl and the two men who have just filled her. The girl's anus is equally available as her sex and Rukimo spreads the slime over that tender hole. The girl barely notices at first. But when Rukimo presents his thick cock, she perks up. She remembers the pain of the assault by the Hispanic man and she tries to dissuade Rukimo in the form of mild but piteous pleas.

But this time, to her surprise, Rukimo's cock slides right in without obstruction. Her widespread legs, the lubrication Rukimo has applied and the fact that her muscles there have not yet retracted to their former state following the assault by Cholo, ease the penetration. It is a whole new experience. The girl discovers that the friction on the ring that surrounds her bottom hole is translated directly to her pussy. The feeling of fullness that Rukimo's large hard cock is giving her is an indescribable sensation. As Rukimo plows away, slowly, but steadily, the girl's passions are aroused once more. She can't believe that she is approaching orgasm in this fashion, but there is no denying her extreme arousal. In the months and years to come, this will become her favorite form of copulation.

As her breath becomes rapid with her approaching orgasm, Rukimo increases the speed and intensity of his strokes. He too is near his peak, but he is holding out so that he can enjoy the girl's mutual release. As she begins to cry out in short, little exclamations, he penetrates her deeply. His cock pulses and spurts its load deep within her. Her eyes have rolled back and she shudders and trembles as the waves of forced pleasure stream over her.

When he is done, Rukimo wipes his cock on a handy towel, removing the brown stains from the girl's bowels. She lies suspended by her legs and her arms, limp and fatigued. Another round of drinks is called for.

While the men refresh themselves, the girl stirs slightly. She is mortified and ashamed of her wanton responses to her nonconsensual use. She looks up. She sees the glow of the fat man's cigar. She cannot make out his features, but can see the outline of his massive form. She realizes that he has been watching the entire time. Rukimo walks over to the man and asks him if he can get him a drink. The man declines. But he instructs Rukimo to have the girl cleaned up and presented to his quarters in an hour. Rukimo responds, "As you wish, Mr. Klitzman."

CHAPTER SIX

TWO WOMEN TAKE A TRIP

I awoke to the sound of a rooster crowing on the porch outside. It wasn't exactly cool, but the sun had not yet heated the muggy air and so it was a comfortable time of day. I saw that the girl still dangled from her rope. "I bet she's got to piss like a race horse," I thought to myself. Well, I did. I stepped back out to the porch and let loose a stream over the balustrade. I didn't know where the cultured gentleman I had met last night usually took his morning ablutions, but this was good enough for me.

I returned inside the house and saw that Morianos was up. He led his 'guest' from the night before by a rope around her neck. She looked much the worse for wear. Morianos looked up at the other girl, still hanging from the rafter.

"Cheeze, gringo," he said. "Didn't you fuck her?"

"I wasn't in the mood," I replied.

"Well, that's your business," he mumbled. "I got to get these bitches ready for the plane. It'll be here in an hour." He pulled out his knife. "Help me get this one down."

I helped Morianos release the well-stretched young woman from her bonds and she slid to the floor. She moved her arms stiffly and looked up at me with disdain. I didn't know if it was because I made her hang there all night or that I had jizzed on her tummy. Either way, she would probably have to keep those kinds of looks to herself in the future.

"Get up you cunt," Morianos yelled at her, kicking her with his foot. "Take off the rest of your clothes. You don't need them anymore."

Less brave now, the girl readily complied with Morianos' orders. She drew her socks and underwear off of her feet. Since her hands were still tied, Morianos assisted her by tearing through her open blouse with his knife. He snipped off the remnants of her bra.

"I'm taking these cunts out to the shithouse. Get yourself some breakfast, you'll be leaving real soon."

The old lady appeared mysteriously with another bowl of chili and a huge hunk of bread. She also brought two more beers. "Well," I thought, "breakfast of champions."

A half hour later, we were heading back to the landing strip. The women were bound hand and foot, naked, in the back seat of the jeep. They were buckled in to prevent escape. Morianos drove. As we arrived, I saw frantic activity at the airstrip. I could now see that the field was a scar cut out of the surrounding jungle. It seemed strange in the early morning light, like some WWII bomber strip hacked out of the jungles of Borneo or New Guinea. While the night before the runway had been deserted, this morning three large trucks had been pulled up and men were unloading them. From two I saw large wooden crates being unloaded. From the third came bundles of plastic covered blocks of white powder. Cocaine.

Within a few minutes of our arrival, a worker

51

pointed up to the sky. We all looked up and saw the large transport circling the field. You would have to be a pretty good pilot to land that thing on this short runway. I assumed that that was what they had.

The plane landed uneventfully. As it taxied up to the loading area, we walked over. Morianos was leading the two stumbling, reticent prisoners by long, leather leashes that had been tied around their throats. Their mouths were gagged as they had been the night before and I could hear their muffled whines and cries as they were pulled along. When we reached the plane, a lanky, blond haired youth emerged from the cabin door. Naturally, he was chewing gum and wearing an obligatory short leather jacket.

"What you got there Morianos, some new customers?" he quipped.

"Yeah," Morianos replied. "Two *gringas* who made a wrong turn. I think the boss will want a word with them."

"Well, bring 'em aboard, we got plenty of room. Is this my other passenger?"

"Yeah, he's a charmer too, like you."

The two men exchanged the banter of workmates. Obviously this guy had made this run many times before. He was nonplussed at the vision of two naked, bound women and so was obviously aware of the nature of their odious future. He also had to know that the men were loading what looked like a ton of cocaine as well as twenty or thirty large wooden crates on his plane. I didn't know what was in the crates, but I was sure that it wasn't anything good.

"Let's get that stuff loaded and gas me up" the

blond kid remarked. "I'm on a schedule you know."

"Yeah, yeah, yeah," said Morianos. "They'll be done quick. In the meantime, why don't you get these two bitches settled?"

Morianos handed the kid the leashes that led to the necks of the women. They must have realized that this was the last opportunity they would have to escape and that getting on the plane would spell their doom. They both dug their heels into the dirt in an effort to resist being pulled into the plane.

Morianos got pissed and started yelling and slapping the girls.

"Cool it Morianos," the kid interjected. "I've got just the thing."

He disappeared momentarily into the plane and emerged with a three-foot long wand. He fiddled with some controls on its side. The women were still resisting and so he reached out with the wand and jabbed it into the rear end of the nearest one. There was a loud 'zap!' and the girl fell down in agony. The other girl stood, shocked, so to speak.

"You all coming in girls or what?" the kid said to the women. Seeing that the alternative to boarding the plane was more of the wand's painful jolts, the women climbed the steps into the plane sullenly.

"That's the good girls," the blond kid said. "Now we'll get you all comfy."

I followed the two women in, carrying my small suitcase. The kid held out his hand. "Jimmy," he said. Jimmy, I thought. It just had to be.

"Yeah," I grumbled back. "Harry." I shook his hand.

The cabin of the plane was small, sitting about ten

people at most. Jimmy sat the women two seats apart from each other in the front row. He pushed them back uncomfortably on their tied hands and belted them in. When he had them settled, he looked at the primitive gags around their mouths. "I've got something better than that," he said.

He went to the back of the cabin and returned with two rubberized hoods. Each sported a spherical tube.

"Watch this," Jimmy said. He removed the gag around the mouth of the first girl, the one who Morianos had tormented the night before. The now desperate woman took the opportunity to beg and plead with this seemingly all American kid.

'Oh, please don't take us. We'll keep quiet. I'm sorry I came here. I won't talk to anyone….."

Jimmy cut her short with a slap across the face.

"Shut up cunt," he said.

The woman quieted, a bright red mark on her cheek. Her eyes were brimming with tears as Jimmy settled the hood around her head. He had some difficulty getting it over her hair, but, it was flexible and he was able to stretch it sufficiently. Once over the top of the head, the hood was pulled down. The woman's frantic eyes disappeared behind the face of the hood. There was a hole for the nose and the rubber sphere was pushed into the girl's mouth. Jimmy linked the straps behind the gag and tightened it in place. The girl was covered from the top of her head to her chin. She shook her head in terrorized frustration. I could hear her mumbled begging and pleading from behind the mask. Jimmy took a small hand pump from his pocket and attached it to a nozzle in the front of the gag, just opposite the mouth. He gave it a few squeezes and the girl bolted upright. Her pleas became panicked murmurs and then were extinguished completely. Jimmy had blown up the rubber ball in her mouth, filling her oral cavity. He snipped off the pump from the nozzle and said, "Voila!"

Only a slight hum could be heard from inside the hood as the girl undoubtedly was attempting to scream frantically from within. Her breasts jiggled nicely as she shook her head and torso futilely.

"Relax, honey," Jimmy told her. "You'll be okay. I promise." He patted her rubber-coated head in reassurance.

Jimmy then turned to the number two girl and removed the cloth gag from her mouth. She said nothing, but she was wide eyed with alarm and shied away as best she could when Jimmy went to apply the hood. She shook her head right and left, making it difficult for him to draw it over her face. Jimmy stood up.

"I'm disappointed in you honey," he said. He reached over and picked up the electrified wand. That was all he had to do. The girl stopped moving her head and whispered plaintively, "Please don't. I'll be good."

Jimmy looked at the girl and then back at the wand as if he was trying to make up his mind whether to zap the girl anyway. She cringed in her seat, expecting the worst. But Jimmy was magnanimous and put the wand down.

When the hood was placed on the second girl and the gag pumped up, Jimmy patted her head as well. He then reached down and took her pale round breasts in his hands. He squeezed them gently, assessing their worth. "Nice tits," was all he said.

He turned to me and told me to make myself comfortable anywhere I wanted. He pointed out the wet bar, a rack of old magazines and a TV and DVD player mounted on the ceiling. "There's some movies in the cabinet there. Help yourself. I've got some sandwiches up front when you get hungry. It's a six hour flight and you may get bored." He started to step into the cabin then stopped and turned around to me. "Let me give you a piece of advice. Don't fuck with the merchandise. Klitzman don't like free lancers. Know what I mean?""

I got Jimmy's gist and nodded my affirmation. As I went to pick out a seat, Morianos came aboard and handed Jimmy a small valise. "This is something special for Rukimo. Don't let anyone else have it or you'll be dead meat," Morianos told him. He also tossed aboard the girls' backpacks, restuffed with their impedimenta. "He'll want to take a look at this stuff too," Morianos added.

He stepped from the plane and closed the outer door. Jimmy went up front to warm the engines. I heard the vast cargo doors to the plane shutting. The engines, twin props on each wing, began to roar and the plane started in motion. I picked out a chair as it lumbered down to the edge of the field. Jimmy made a wide turn at the end of the runway and stopped the plane. He looked back at me through the cabin door.

"Here's the fun part," he said. "Hope you have a Will."

The engines began to roar mightily. I could feel the

plane trying to move forwards, held back I supposed by the brakes. Suddenly, with a jerk, the plane lurched and started its run. I decided I had to see for myself and so I crept forwards to the door of the cockpit where I could see out the windscreen. The trees at the end of the runway were getting closer and closer. The plane was going faster and faster. And yet I felt no rise in the wings, no lifting off of the ground. I grabbed the edges of the doorway and held on for dear life. My knuckles turned white, my mouth got dry. Suddenly, the plane jerked upwards. Jimmy had lowered the flaps. Almost as if in slow motion, the plane rose steadily. I swore I could hear the branches of the trees at the end of the runway scraping our wheels as we got fully into the air.

"Well," Jimmy laughed, "I did it again!"

CHAPTER SEVEN

A GIRL IS SOLD

The French girl's body was being meticulously examined by a tall, thin, dark skinned man. He wore a long white cotton caftan and a maroon turban on his head. He was accompanied by a small, fat fellow who was similarly dressed. The girl was naked, her hands held behind her head, her legs spread.

It had been several months since she had found herself a captive of the cruel men who had whipped and raped her. Her brand had healed and the bright red "K" on her rear was now a permanent fixture on her body. The slight baby fat she had exhibited on her first day was gone, replaced with taut, firm muscles. Her light tan had faded, and her skin now was as white as alabaster.

The thin man lifted her breasts, squeezing them gently. He spoke some words in Arabic to his partner. The partner, meanwhile, was rubbing his hands over her rear, remarking the deep gouge that had been made by the brand. He reached from behind the girl and rubbed the now hairless sex. The girl made no protest at his handling of her, only a slight intake of breath as the fat man jammed a finger into her pussy.

She had been well trained. It had taken much pain and suffering on her part to understand that her old life was over forever. She had to acknowledge her new status as owned property. She had to open herself to all who desired her and to engage in whatever acts they demanded. She had, at the urging of a whip, learned to take cocks down her throat, to lick and suck on them as if every moment that one violated her mouth was a moment of ecstasy. Her rear and sex had been plundered uncounted times until she learned how to move her body to give maximum joy to her possessors. And she learned to stand still, when ordered to, to remain silent unless spoken to, and to address all males as her master.

Her English lessons had been perfunctory. "Spread your legs", "open your mouth", "kneel", were some of the few words of English that she was specifically taught. She had picked up some more like, "slut", "whore", and "pussy" on her own.

The girl had stopped crying after about two weeks. At that point hopelessness took its toll. At first, she had thought she was a lonely prisoner of these evil men. But after the first day, she saw that there were more women, imprisoned, branded, whipped and beaten like she was. They brought her another young French girl, a tiny thing, with small breasts and welts all over her body. She translated the big black man's instructions to her on deportment and the purpose of her presence. Thus, she learned that she had become enslaved; that she would not see France again, not see her family, her friends, not walk freely in the sun, not dance at her favorite clubs, eat at her favorite cafes. Most importantly, she learned that she was now an owned object, no more than an animal of pleasure.

Now, the tall man examined the inside of her

mouth, looked into her eyes. "They buy horses like this," she thought. He took his turn at examining her pussy, rubbing the tender tip of her clitoris with his long, boney fingers until it stood, engorged. He ran his fingers down her cleft, feeling her wetness as her vulva opened. She had learned to respond to the touches of strange men. The whip had taught her that. She learned to take her mind to a place where sexual pleasure would flow. She did it now, knowing that the lash would follow if she was found wanting.

Satisfied at his examination, the tall man stepped away from the slender, curvaceous French girl. He turned to sit at a small, low table, crossing his legs. The fat man stood behind him. Rukimo, the black man who had assaulted her on her first day, was there.

She could not understand the words, but she had guessed at the purpose of her examination. She was to be sold.

"As you have said," the tall man began in Arabic, "she is a delightful specimen. She is all as you described, beautiful."

"I sell your master only the best," the big black man said. "And she is well trained."

"I could see that by the lushness of her cleft as I rubbed it. My master wants female slaves that will show real passion when stimulated."

"She has learned to show passion whether she feels it or not," the black man retorted. "Do you want me to make her come?"

"It will not be necessary. I know that if my master is displeased you will take her back."

"Of course. And she knows that if she is sent back it

will go very badly for her."

The tall man took a sip of tea. "You have set your price and in these matters my master does not like to haggle. He will remit your fee in the usual way."

"Good," the black man replied. "I will have her packaged and ready within the hour."

From the conclusive tone of the conversation between the men, the French girl knew that she had been sold. To what cruel master would she now belong? Whoever it was and wherever he took her, she would be one more step removed from her home, one more step removed from freedom.

She was taken down to a room below the room where she had been displayed for sale. There, three of the ubiquitous black robed African supervisors were waiting for her. A knot had formed in her stomach. The past months had been a tortuous journey from innocence to depravity. She had been beaten and abused many times. But she had learned to live within the rules. She had learned when to accept instructions docilely and when to energetically apply her new found whorish skills. Now, she was going to an unknown destination. Some of the men she had serviced while on this small African island had been demanding indeed. Some enjoyed the torture of a young woman for its own sake. Had she been sold to one of those men? Would her daily life be one of constant torture and fear? How long could she survive and still be a person?

These questions rushed through the girl's mind as she was made to kneel. She trembled as a leather hood was forced over her head. It was designed to block all light and hearing from its wearer. A last thought of struggle, as vain as it might be, shot across her mind as the hood descended over her eyes. But it was too late even for that. As the hood slipped into place, the girl was irremediably isolated from the world around her. A rubber gag was stuffed into her mouth and affixed to the outer portion of the hood. Her hands were locked behind her.

Effectively reduced to an anonymous object, she was led to a toilet and, as she had practiced many times, peed when her labia were stroked appropriately. She was douched so that her pussy would arrive at her new home fresh. She was given an enema to prevent an untoward accident on her trip.

Her packaging was simple, but effective. She was made to sit on a base with two dildos attached, one taller and thicker than the other. One of the supervisors carefully aligned them to her sex and rear. They easily slid into place, as they had been greased and, as the girl had been trained, she relaxed her muscles to ease their penetration. Her legs were crossed in front of her and strapped to the base on which she sat. The sides of the crate were now added. Foam pillows were packed tightly around her body to prevent movement. A long tube was run through her gag and into her mouth to facilitate breathing. Its other end was affixed to a special nozzle in the top of the crate.

As the top of the crate was affixed, the girl began to panic. She had suffered her packaging passively, almost serenely, but when she felt the vibration of the top being put in place, she realized that her only link to life was the thin little tube that ran through her gag. Her bonds were too strong and severe to permit any movement except a slight nodding of her head. As she felt the cool air of the room outside her little prison fill her lungs through the little tube, she felt relieved, or as relieved as an enslaved female could be under the circumstances.

The sides of the crate had two handles and it was easy to lift it onto a small dolly. She was wheeled to an elevator and brought up to ground level. As the small, black box appeared, the agents of her new master were waiting and, after shaking the big black man's hand and exchanging kisses on the cheeks, they stepped outside and entered the van that would drive them to the airstrip. The crate was loaded into the back. The van drove away.

CHAPTER EIGHT

HARRY'S EDUCATION BEGINS

As the plane touched down somewhere off the coast of Africa, I contemplated my dilemma. Here I was landing in the middle of god knows where, with a future very much in doubt. The things that Morianos had said about Klitzman's island were intriguing to say the least. But what would be my role? Would I ever be contacted by the "Agency" whoever they were?

Our landing was smooth, and as soon as it came to a halt the door was opened from the outside. A large, black man outfitted in a black and red uniform, a huge sidearm and a baton that would have delighted Harmon Killebrew, came aboard. His red and black striped, short sleeve shirt was starched and pressed to razor sharp creases. The uniform pants carried a red stripe down the sides. His cap was peaked and had a wide, plastic brim. He motioned me to sit while he unstrapped the two women from their seats. He dragged them unceremoniously to the door where they were led out by another dark, heavy fellow. I was then invited off the plane.

As I went through the doorway, the heat and humidity hit me like a wet sponge in the face. We were in Africa all right. It was nighttime and the whole place was lit up like a ballpark. I could make out a cyclone fence behind the lights, but no other identifying

64

features. There was a small hut about 200' from where we were with two vehicles standing outside. The first was a small van standing closest to the hut. Next to the van was one of those limos you saw taking movie stars to Hollywood or Atlantic City. As we walked to the hut, I saw the two naked and hooded women being trundled into the back door of the van. The door shut and it sped away. I was led into the hut.

"Please undress and place all of your clothes in the bags," spoke the guard who had led me in. "You will then please put on this robe and sandals." I complied in silence. The robe was made of light cotton and wrapped around my front. It was tied shut with a belt of similar material that wrapped around my body twice. The robe was a bright yellow color, which kind of made me feel like an overstuffed banana. My little suitcase, whatever it contained, was taken from me. I had never opened it.

I walked out to the waiting limo. As soon as I got in, it moved off. The limo exited the tarmac after crossing through a well-guarded gate. We then rode for about a half hour before we came to another gate. There were more armed guards there and they had me get out of the van and examined me with their flashlights. One of them was carrying a picture that I assumed was me. The men all looked at it and then at me and we were then waived through the gate.

About ten minutes later we pulled up to another gate. The limo was admitted and then stopped so that I could get out. When got out I could see that I was between two steel fences, both topped with barbed wire and, I guessed, electrified. There was a small hut that sat between the two fences. The driver motioned me to follow him. I entered the small hut and stood in front of a large, heavy footed, colonial style desk. The driver handed what I took to be some form of pass to another guard sitting at the desk and walked back outside. I could hear the limo pulling away. The guard behind the desk looked at the pass and at me and shrugged. He handed it back to me. "Walk through that door," he said, "and follow the path to the next building. You will be welcomed there and your processing will begin".

I did as I was told. I felt like I was trying to get into Fort Knox. The path was about four feet wide and lined by 12' high steel fencing on each side. It was about 20 yards long and led to a large white stone building, two stories, built in a modern style with sleek, low lines and nestled into the hillside. I walked in through a large steel door. A small, dark Caucasian man was standing there, waiting for me. He had short, black hair and was about forty and in good shape. He reached out his right hand in greeting. "My name is Anthony," he said. "I'll be handling your orientation session here tonight. Tomorrow morning you'll be allowed inside, but tonight, we're going to take some medical tests, get you filled in on the rules and get you some rest. Please come with me."

I followed Anthony through the foyer and through another steel door, which led into the interior of the building. He led me to a series of small rooms, and instructed me to wait inside one of them. I entered the third door and sat down on a small examination table that was set against the wall, the only furniture in the room. After about a half hour, the door opened and a slight, middle-aged Asian man, also wearing a red robe, came in pushing a small cart. "I am going to take some blood, a urine specimen and your fingerprints, sir. Then you will wait here until Anthony comes back for you." I permitted him to take the blood sample and fingerprints and then pissed into a small jar he gave me.

Obviously, the club took no chances on a man's health or his identity. The technician left the room and about a half hour later the door reopened. It was Anthony. "Come on, let's go on upstairs," he said. "A nice meal, some conversation and then beddie bye."

"Listen, what is this crap. I'm no tourist here and I'm about..." I was trying to assert myself.

"Whoa, relax Mr. Wiggins," Anthony interrupted patiently. "You'll be taken care of. Everybody's got to go through this when they come in from the outside. SOP, you know."

"Yeah, well I don't like this shit, you understand, all this barbed wire and guards make me feel like I'm back at the joint."

"Believe me, Mr. Wiggins," Anthony continued, "prison was never like this. Just wait until tomorrow."

"Okay, okay," I said. "I've been on the road it seems forever. And I haven't had a good meal since I got locked up."

"Sure, that's where we're going now."

"Just do me a favor?"

"If I can," Anthony replied.

"Don't call me Mr. Wiggins, only judges, cops and prosecutors call me that."

"Sure, Harry, sure," he responded, smiling.

We dined in a small room, elegantly appointed. Dinner was a spicy chowder made from local seafood and a sixteen-ounce N.Y. cut sirloin. Anthony served the dishes after getting them from a dumbwaiter located in the wall. The wine was a delightful red Bordeaux. We ate in silence and, after we were done, I was led down a short corridor to a series of doors that led to bedrooms.

"Normally, we have more than one guest arriving," Anthony told me. "But tonight it's just you. Make yourself comfortable and I'll see you in the morning."

I stepped into the room indicated by Anthony for me, took a short but delightful shower and then spread myself out on the full size bed located against the wall opposite the door. I was asleep in seconds.

The next morning I woke suddenly and with a start. Anxiously, for about 10 seconds, I wondered where I was. As my head cleared, I realized that the meal the night before must have been doctored with a mild sedative. I looked around the room. There was no window and the door had no handle. There was a small table next to the door, which had a telephone on it. I walked over and picked up the receiver. A voice responded, "Yes, Mr. Wiggins?"

"When do I get out of here?"

"Shortly, sir. First, I'll have breakfast sent in."

The door opened about ten minutes later and a beauteous young woman stood there holding a tray. On it was a melon, some toast and a thermos of coffee. As a black robed guard held the door open, she entered my room and set the tray down on the nightstand. The guard closed the door and the two of us were left standing there.

The girl was young, about 21 or 22 years old. Her

hair was long and black. It was flat and straight and descended halfway down her back. She was not slender, but seemed properly proportioned for her height, about 5'6". She was utterly naked except for the leather collar that she wore around her neck and the leather bracelets around her wrists and ankles. She was barefooted.

She looked down at the floor, her head bowed. Her hands were placed behind her, her feet were set wide apart. A well-trimmed bush, just big enough to be bikini sized, framed her pussy.

Breakfast seemed a dull proposition after seeing this girl in my room. My cock had taken a life of its own and peeked out from my robe. I didn't know what to say to this girl. I started out the normal way.

"What's your name?"

She replied in a low, almost whispered voice. "My name, if it pleases the master, is Adriana."

Her voice was thickly accented. Judging by her black hair and the dark tones of her skin, I guessed that she was Italian or Greek.

"And what am I to do with you, Adriana?" I asked her.

"Whatever the master desires," she answered.

I longed to touch her generous breasts and to put my lips on her skin. "Come closer to me, Adriana,"

The girl stepped closer so that she stood about six inches from my body. I reached out my hand and stroked her gleaming black hair. She had been lightly perfumed, a kind of jasmine scent. I breathed her in with passionate delight. I realized that she was looking directly down at my cock, the head of which had sprung free from my robe.

"May I pleasure you, master?" she asked timidly.

"I would like that, Adriana," I said.

The girl fell to her knees and parted my robe. She took my cock in her hands and gently covered its head with her lips. I felt a tingling in my flesh as her kiss of my prick went directly to my brain. I leaned back so that I was resting on the nightstand. Adriana opened her mouth and swallowed my cock.

I closed my eyes and let the young girl pleasure me. She stroked my balls as she glided her tongue up and down my shaft. I groaned with pleasure.

In spite of the exquisite oral attention to my manhood, I could not but think that in spite of this girl's apparent eagerness to pleasure me, she was a slave, a sexual slave. Nothing that she did was of her own free will. The grounds for her energetic administrations to my cock had been laid at some time before, enforced by the crack of a whip.

It did not take long for me to deliver a load of my thick, white cum into the girl's mouth. She swallowed it dutifully as she coaxed the last drop out with her lips. My mind reeled from the pleasurable sensations sent to it by my throbbing cock. It had been a long time.

I pulled my cock back from her mouth and went to sit on the bed, my body still reverberating with the tremors of my orgasm. She knelt before me, head down, hands behind her. I was astounded at my first encounter with one of Klitzman's slaves. The way she carried herself, held her body open to my gaze, knelt poised in anticipation of an order or command from me, reignited my desire. I wanted to fuck her.

"Get up on the bed," I ordered.

She scrambled on top of the bed and turned to face me. Her eyes were wide apart, a deep brown, almost black. She had full lips that seemed poised for use. I took a breast in my hand and squeezed it softly. As I kneaded the nipple with my fingers, I felt it getting hard. I pushed the girl over onto her back and slid myself next to her. I seized her left breast with my lips and sucked at it gently. My cock was stirring once again. I ran my hand down the girl's taut, firm stomach and covered her sex, grasping it, cupping it in my palm. As I slid my fingers into her crevasse, I felt that she was lubricated, her lips parting easily. I rubbed her clit with my thumb, she sighed, her eyes closing. I insinuated myself between her thighs and presented my hard cock to her moist lower lips. She spread her legs and thrust her hips forwards invitingly. Slowly, languidly, I eased my cock into her passage, relishing the warmth and softness I found there.

It had been over three and a half years since I had penetrated a pussy with my cock. I had almost forgotten the intensity of the pleasure of having my manhood surrounded by warm, tender flesh. As I reached deep into her, the girl began to move her hips. I could feel her cunt tighten around me and I sighed heavily.

Slowly, but surely, the tempo of my thrusts increased. The girl was now uttering little cries each time I dragged my cock against her engorged bud of pleasure. I felt her arms around my back, her legs intertwining mine as she tried to pull me deeper inside her. Suddenly, my cock began to throb, spurting my second discharge of the day into her deep recesses. The girl pushed against me with her hips and cried out. Her shudders and moans indicated to me that she too had reached climax.

After a few moments of afterglow, I disentangled myself from the slave girl and sat back and stared at her. Her expression had not changed. It was still a neutral, emotionless demeanor. But I could see from the listlessness of her body that she was relishing the sense of relaxation that an orgasm brings.

After a moment, there was a knock on the door. I answered, "Yes. Come in."

The door opened and Anthony stuck in his head.

"Ready to go?" he asked. Then, seeing my naked form and the girl's splayed body he added, "I see you favored sex over breakfast this morning. Adriana is a delightful slave; I'm not surprised."

Still looking intently at the slave girl's face, I acknowledged his estimation of the girl. "She's a good fuck," I said. "Is she yours?"

"Oh, no, she belongs to the club, at least for now. Later she might be sold, but right now there's too many who like her. I get her assigned down here whenever I can. In fact...," his voice raised an octave, his tone became stern. "Adriana, get up and go tell the duty supervisor that I want to have you tonight."

"Yes, master," Adriana replied as she shimmied off of the bed. As she passed me, I grabbed her by the waist and pulled her to me once more. I placed my lips on her nipples and kissed them, one after the other.

"Thank you, Adriana," I said.

She looked up at me strangely. "Y-yes, Master," she replied. And then she scooted from the room.

I was sitting there buck naked, my banana robe on a hook behind the door. My flaccid cock pointed to the floor. "There's a red robe for you in the closet," Anthony said.

I donned the red robe and let Anthony lead me down the hall.

"What's with the colored robes," I asked.

"It's so we can keep track of who's who. Red robes are for supervisors, like me, and now you. Blue is for guests. Black is for security. The service staff, cooks, cleaners, slave tenders, they wear white uniforms. The girl's, of course, wear nothing."

"And banana?" I asked.

Anthony laughed. "Yellow is for newcomers who haven't been processed. No one gets in without a full medical checkup. We wouldn't want anyone coming down with anything nasty."

"So, where do we go from here?" I asked.

"Well, you have to meet with Rukimo. He's the head honcho around here, second only to Mr. Klitzman. But first, I want to show you around a little."

When we got to the end of the hallway, we passed through a doorway and into another hall. There was a black robed guard standing there at attention at the end. Anthony pulled out a small card, showed it to the guard who then opened the door with a key that was fastened to a leather thong attached to his belt. We walked through and stepped out onto a large terrace. Strewn about the terrace were a number of tables and chairs, some of them occupied by blue and red clad figures. We walked past the tables and I noticed that on the ground next to one or two of them were kneeling women, naked, their arms crossed behind them, their eyes downcast. Slaves. "Staff and guests mix pretty freely," Anthony commented. "When you talk to them you can tell them about your life of crime, I'm sure it will fascinate them. But we are on a first name only basis here. Don't give your last name or how you got here. And never get soused in the guest areas. It doesn't look good and you never know what might happen." This was like having a big brother.

I could feel a moderately cool breeze blowing from the ocean, which was overlooked by the terrace. On the beach I could see various figures, some swimming, some on the strand. I saw one guy who looked like he was humping a girl right out in the open. He was.

Anthony took me through a set of double doors that led into a large area containing a bar, some couches and chairs and a stage in the middle. The air conditioning felt good, even with the breeze outside. This tropical weather was going to take some getting used to. On the stage was a brown skinned girl dangling from a chain that hung from the ceiling. Several naked women were kneeling along the walls of the room, their hands held palms up, resting on their thighs. Anthony led me over to a dark haired girl, pale, with large, rounded breasts. Her head was bent over, eyes cast downwards. Her posture was perfect, shoulders back, back straight, thighs apart. "This is one of my favorite slaves, Maria. A little Italian girl. I just want you to see how the girls are outfitted."

The girl had a leather collar around her neck, which was attached to the wall by a thin chain. Her wrists were enclosed by leather bracelets, as were her ankles.

Her black hair was cut short with large ringlets of curls. She wore light makeup around her eyes and a dark red lipstick. She was gorgeous. "As you can see, the chain is attached to the collar with a small lock. Guests are all given keys which fit the collars and bracelets, as well as most of the chains and body locks used in the guest area." Anthony lifted up the chin of the Italian girl and squeezed her face tightly. A look of pain crossed it. And fear. "There is still a punishment owed to this slave. Perhaps I will tend to it this evening." The girl visibly shuddered.

Anthony led me past the bar and through a doorway that led to a hall lined with doors. Each one was marked with a small card with the occupant's first name and last name initial. Several guests passed us in the hallway, each saying hello to me and Anthony. Quite jolly. One fellow was leading a tall, slender girl with a hood over her head. The chain was affixed to a ring under her chin. Her hands were bound to her sides to a wide belt around her middle. I could see welts across her thighs. The guest stopped in front of us.

"I want to report an infraction," the guest said to Anthony. "This girl was slow to obey and she attempted to resist when being whipped." The guest was about 6'2", 220 pounds. It was hard to imagine this girl resisting him for a minute.

"Well, Paul, do you want us to report her or should we take her for discipline now?" Anthony asked.

"Take her now," Paul said, "I'd like to have her back tonight."

"Fine. Harry, would you mind taking this slave's leash and bringing her along."

I grabbed the leash from Paul the moose and followed Anthony down the hall. The girl stumbled behind me. It was quite a new sensation to have such power over a woman. All of these women. I felt like I was in some kind of movie or dream. "This can't be real," I thought. Not only were all of the women young and pleasing to the eye, but their subservience was apparent by their very demeanor. Their eyes were uniformly downcast, their bodies were posed lasciviously, breasts held high and proud, thighs open. My cock was a stiff as a board as I led the comely slave down the hall. I presumed that having me tow the girl along was Anthony's way of getting me into the swing of things. I have to say that I needed little encouragement.

The hallway curved in a semicircle that terminated in a glass atrium doorway, which led outside. There were thirty guest rooms. Across a small courtyard was another atrium style door marked by red and brown stripes along the floor and around the door. Staff areas. We entered the door and were greeted by a guard. Anthony showed him his pass card and we were admitted.

"I'll get you your pass after lunch. First let's take this slave down to a holding area. We can discipline her after I show you your room and get you fixed up."

We walked past a series of doors and then through a large commons area. Several staff members were there drinking coffee, bullshitting. There were a few girls scattered around the room, some kneeling, some standing and one mounted on a platform in the middle of the room. She had long brown hair, which fell about her face as she knelt there on all fours. There were stripes on her rear. A staff member sitting in an easy chair was absentmindedly caressing the breast of a girl kneeling by his side while he talked to a supervisor across from him.

After we exited the commons area, we approached a series of chains dangling from the wall. Anthony commanded the girl to kneel and he chained her neck to the wall, leaving her only about six inches of play. The girl was facing the wall. Anthony took a small book from his pocket and checked the girl's collar. There was a small disk hanging from the back with a number on it. Anthony wrote it down in his book.

We left the girl and proceeded down the hallway. We stopped at the fifth door. It had the name Harry W. on a small card next to the door. My room. We walked in. "There aren't any locks on any of the doors," Anthony told me. "What we do here is perfectly open to everyone else. No one has any property, so there's nothing to steal. As a matter of courtesy, no one goes into anyone else's room uninvited unless on official business. But it's the principal that counts."

There was a girl in the middle of the room kneeling with her arms resting on her thighs, just like the girls in the guests' commons. Rest position, I was to learn. "This is your attendant," Anthony advised me. "As a staff member, you are entitled to an attendant full time. Unlike the guests, you may reserve her exclusively for up to a week. Then she has to go back into the pool. She will tend to your personal needs and show you where your clothes and personal items are kept."

Anthony spoke to the slave, "Have you been given a

name?"

"Yes Master" she answered without looking up. She spoke with a distinct accent. Not French. Maybe Dutch?

"Well, what is it?" Anthony demanded.

"Tulip, master." she answered. Dutch it was.

Anthony turned to me. "Of course, you may call her what you wish. She has been instructed to maintain your room and to tend to her own personal needs without further orders. Food will be delivered to her by servants on a regular basis. When not servicing you or the room or attending to personal needs, and unless you give her alternative orders, she will return to this position after doing her duties. It is necessary that you discipline your attendant well. Frequently we use slaves who are in the last steps of their training as body servants. Part of your job is to complete their training so that they will please the guests properly. Come on, drop your suitcase and we'll go see Rukimo."

I dropped off my suitcase and ordered the girl to put my things away. Not my things really, just some stuff they had given me. But it was all I had.

We left Tulip sitting in the rest position as we departed the room. We walked back out to the commons area, passing the tall girl from before. One of the staff members had put on some music and the girl on the dais rose to her feet and began to move gracefully in time to the luxurious beat of the music. It was a cool jazz number, with a sinewy saxophone riff and a heavy beat.

Anthony turned to me and said, "Watch this."

I stood mesmerized as the girl rolled her graceful,

inviting hips to the beat of the music. All eyes in the room were on her. Her long brown hair flowed around her as she turned and dipped her knees. Her face was aglow with passion as if the music had triggered a burning lust within her.

I watched as the lithe, brown skinned girl began to caress the twin globes of delightful flesh on her chest. She licked her lips with her long tongue and pulled on her nipples, extending her breasts from her body. Her eyes were alight and darted from face to face in the room. She seemed to draw energy from the lust that she was generating. After raising herself to her full height and running her hands down her sides, she slowly lowered her body, her hips gyrating to the now pounding rhythm of the drums. The saxophone wailed as if tormented by her tantalizing movements.

When her knees reached the dais, the girl leaned back, touching the floor behind her with her hands. Her legs were spread and the lips of her sex glistened with her incumbent passion. She rolled over and pressed her forehead down, raising her ass high, her back curved like the string of a taut bow. A hand snaked between her legs and delved into the wet slit between them. Still moving to the beat of the music, rocking her hips from side to side, she began to stroke herself.

I had to resist pulling out my cock and running up to the stage. I glanced around the room and several of the men had slave girls on their laps, their legs spread wide, and had their hands up the girl's slits. One girl was on her knees servicing a short, but muscular bald headed guy. His robe was spread open and his eyes were closed, delighting in the mouth that had fastened itself on his prick. Anthony's eyes were glued to the spectacle of the swaying, squirming brown haired dancer.

She had begun to moan. She rolled onto her back, spreading her legs wide to their extreme and plunged her fingers into her pussy. Her back was arched and she thrust her hips in time with her hand's exertions. As the song wound down, she began to cry out. Her skin was wet with sweat, sparkling under the overhead spotlight. The song ended, the sax fading to a whisper until the only sound in the room was the girl's cries of ecstasy as she orgasmed right on the stage. If it was a fake, it was very, very good. I doubted whether even a well-trained girl could make her pussy gush on command. I could see a small puddle of her juices that had dripped from her flushed and engorged pussy lips.

A man rushed up and, grabbing her head, rammed his cock into her mouth. She sucked at it hungrily as another man rose to stuff her soft, dilated sex. The lust generated by the girl had spread through the room like an epidemic, as all around slave girls were being plowed fore and aft. I must have made some involuntary move towards one of the girls when Anthony grabbed my sleeve.

"Whoa, boy," he said, amused. "We're on our way to see Rukimo, remember?"

I turned to him, startled out of the trance that the dancing girl had put me in. "Ah, yeah," was all I could say.

Anthony started to walk away. I reluctantly followed.

CHAPTER NINE

HER NEW HOME

The young French girl had been locked in her mobile prison for many hours. She had been given a mild soporific before she had been packaged for shipment and so, for much of the time, she had floated in and out of consciousness. She had felt it when her box had been lifted from the van and carried by forklift to the waiting airplane. She had noted the unmistakable sensations of taking off. But she had not been able to give them much thought as her mind quickly clouded over. The faint sounds of the plane's engines and its graceful yawing were lulling.

After a couple of hours, the girl gradually resumed full consciousness. The terrible reality of what had happened to her struck home like the blow from a fist. She had inured herself to her fate through her months of training and service on Klitzman's island. Her whippings, the rapes, the abusive objectification she had suffered, had driven her emotions deep within her. She suppressed all thoughts of her former life and dealt only with thoughts of how to avoid pain, how to serve her masters. But now the terrible nature of her fate caused her to rediscover her fear and terror as well as the loneliness and despair of someone torn irremediably from their safe and comfortable life.

Tears flowed down her face for the first time in

many months. She remembered her family, her friends. Did they remember her? Did they wonder at her fate? Would she ever laugh again? Locked and trussed in a box, naked, impaled by steel hard shafts, flying to some unknown destination, it seemed doubtful indeed. Who would her new master be? What cruelties would he inflict on her?

As she felt the airplane begin its descent, the girl knew that her future would soon be known.

When the plane landed, a black van rolled over the tarmac to meet it. The imprisoned girl was quickly off loaded from the plane and placed in the van's rear. It sped away.

Property of the Emir was immune from customs search. The van turned onto the airport highway and made its way to the Palace compound. Located outside of the busy commercial center of the Emirate, the Palace sat miles into the hinterland. It took forty-five minutes for the van to make the trip at a very high speed. Once in the gates of the compound, the van rolled to the freight dock and the box was lifted out and placed on a dolly. It was rolled inside, through the Palace's warehouse and directly into the living quarters.

The French girl had another hour to wait before there was any change in her status. She knew that she had arrived at her destination but, of course, still had no clue as to what awaited her. After an hour, the box was rolled down a long hallway, taken down an elevator and then down another long hallway. The girl could sense the opening of her tiny prison. As her hood was removed, her eyes were shocked by the sudden infusion of light. She saw hands reaching in, strong masculine hands, untying the cords that had held her immobile for so long. She was lifted delicately off of the intruders in her sex and rear and removed from the box.

The girl was laid on the floor, her legs gently extended. She was rolled over to her stomach so that the bindings on her wrists could be undone. Her gag was released. She was stunned by this frenetic activity after so long in stasis. The men who were handling her were dressed in white cotton shirts and khaki pants. Their faces and skin were mauve. Their hands and arms were strong. They worked silently.

After the strong hands had massaged her arms and legs to encourage circulation, the girl was pulled to her feet. Bracelets were quickly affixed to her wrists behind her back and a leather ball shoved into her mouth. A black bag descended over her head.

The men led the girl back down the hall and up the elevator. She was dragged down a hallway, through two sets of doors and then into a large, pushily carpeted room. For ten minutes, she stood there expectantly.

Suddenly she heard a shriek and feminine laughter.

"Oh, she's here, she's here!" a voice cried out in Arabic. It was the Emir's First Wife, Damira, a fortyish, black haired, rotund woman. With her was the Emir's First Daughter, the Princess Alliyah, a delicate, gracefully formed young girl of 18 years. The French girl, of course, could not understand a word they said.

"Oh, she's beautiful mother," the young girl exclaimed. "I want to touch her, may I?"

"Of course, little flower, of course," the Queen replied. "But let's see her face; I want to see her face!"

One of the servants quickly removed the girl's hood.

The two women cooed in admiration. "She's wonderful," the Queen exclaimed. "Exactly what we wanted."

Alliyah approached the French girl cautiously. She extended her hand and delicately caressed the French girl's cheek. The girl was surprised by her reception. She had not expected to see women, and free women to boot. She could see from their raiment that they were wealthy, important women. The sight of joyful, laughing women was crushing to her. She stood naked, bound, a slave, before women who breathed free air, who had the right to wear beautiful clothes, to talk freely, to express their humanity.

The French girl grimaced at the soft touch of the beautiful, young girl. She began to cry.

"Oh, you've frightened her," the Queen said to her daughter. "She's been through a lot. Be careful with her."

"I'll be careful, mother," the Princess replied. "But I want to touch her. She's like a delicate bird."

As the Queen waved the servants away, the Princess stepped up to the trembling girl. She placed her soft hands on the girl's shoulders and ran them down her arms. "Her skin is soft, mother. And her breasts are so pretty. I'm jealous."

"Now let me see her, Alliyah, I'm the one who bought her," the Queen interjected.

The Princess moved aside to let her mother have access.

"Oh, yes, her breasts are fine," she said as she reached out to stroke them. She measured their weight and firmness in her hands. "They're the perfect size."

She grabbed the slave girl's cheeks with her hand and examined her face closely. She took her time, looking for blemishes, any defect that would mar her new property. Her hand was strong and the girl trembled as she feared for her future. Had she been bought to serve this callous woman? The girl? Would they whip her?

"A lovely face," the mother concluded happily. "Rashid has a wonderful eye for women. Her eyes are delicate, a beautiful green. I like that." The Queen released the French girl's face. With a lightening stroke, she slapped her hard across the face.

"Mother!" the Princess called out as the 'crack' echoed throughout the room.

The French girl was startled by the suddenness of the blow. It stung harshly. Losing all memory of what was forbidden, her eyes lit up with resentment and hatred.

"Ah," the Queen said. "She has spirit. Good." She swung her other hand around and another 'crack' resounded.

"Mother, what are you doing?" the Princess exclaimed.

The girl cringed now, expecting yet another blow. The Queen answered her daughter, "She needs to know what's what, my dear. You have to be harsh with a slave before you are kind. Kindness has to purchased by obedience. Believe me, I have broken in many a slave for your father."

"Please don't hit her again," the Princess implored.

"I don't intend to," the Queen answered. "I just wanted to get that out of the way."

The French girl tried to shy away as the Queen's

hands returned to her breasts, but the guards held her still. The Queen pulled sharply on her fear hardened nipples. The girl's face cringed in pain. The Queen smiled. "Oh, she's a sensitive one. But let's see the rest of her."

She ordered the guards to turn her around. The Princess saw the bright red "*k*" branded on her rear. She reached out and placed her fingers in the depression that had been burned into the slave girl's skin. "That's so pretty," she said. "But I bet it hurt."

"Like the blazes, daughter," the Queen answered. She took a handful of the soft flesh on the girl's rear. "Soft, but firm," she remarked. She spoke to the guards, "Let her go. We'll call you when we want you."

The guards bowed to the Queen and the Princess and withdrew from the room. The Queen grabbed one of the girl's arms and led her to a long, low, backless couch. Sitting down, she pulled the girl on to her lap and then pushed her down on her back. Grabbing her knees, she spread the girl's legs.

All of the handling of her breasts and rear had induced the girl's sex to lubricate. Her body had been trained to prepare itself for invasion when stroked by a master. The tender lips glistened as they were forced open by the spread of her legs. A small patch of black hair perched above her delicate divide and a tiny line of shortly trimmed bristle graced the swelling lips.

"Mama!" the young Princess exclaimed.

"Oh, hush," she replied. "I want to see her pussy. It's lovely, don't you think?"

"Mama!" the embarrassed Princess replied.

"Haven't you ever looked closely at a cunt, my dear?

Come, take a good look. If it wasn't for cunts men would ignore us."

The Princess giggled. "Can I touch it?"

"Of course, sweetheart. Have a good feel."

Extending her hand timidly, the Princess knelt next to the prone slave and placed her fingers on the now engorged lips. She looked up at her mother.

"Go on, go on," her mother said. "Have a good feel. Put your fingers inside and tickle her clit. See if you can make her moan."

The French girl felt the long, slender fingers of the Princess enter her. She sighed as they slid along the walls of her impassioned tunnel. The fingers delved deep inside her causing her to shudder. Alliyah placed her thumb on the sensitive, hardened button at the apex of the girl's sex and rubbed it gently. The girl moaned.

The Queen laughed. "She's a hot one!" she exclaimed. "Here, let get her up."

The Princess stepped back and, grabbing the girl's arm, helped her mother bring her to a sitting position. The Queen pulled the surprised slave girl back onto her lap, spread her legs and delved into the now hot sex. "Watch," she told her daughter.

With one arm around the girl's back, the Queen caressed the slave girl's wet gash. She watched the slave girl's face intently, as did the Princess. The French girl's breath began to shorten as she was induced into a passionate trance. Her skin sparkled with perspiration, her breasts hardened. The Queen brought her to the brink of explosion and withdrew her hand. The girl's eyes gazed at the Queen imploringly. The Queen smiled.

"Kiss her nipples, my little flower," she told her daughter. "See how she moans."

Uncertainly, the Princess leaned over, squatting next to her mother and placed her lips on the tight, hard dart atop the girl's left breast. She kissed it tenderly, surprised at the salty taste and the pull she felt in her own loins. Encouraged, the Princess sucked at the teat, first softly, and then harder. The French girl moaned, a long, deep, blissful moan.

The Queen resumed her manipulation of the slave girl's hot sex. The girl trembled, breathing hard now,

"Watch her face, watch her face," the Queen excitedly told her daughter. "Watch her while she comes!"

The Princess watched, mesmerized as little cries eked out of the French girl's mouth, stifled not fully by the ball of leather within. Louder and louder the cries came as the girl came closer and closer to release. Finally, with a loud moan, the girl's thighs and body began to tremor. Her chest heaved, shaking her breasts. "Uh! Uh! Uh! Uh!" she called out as the pulsing of her pussy subsumed her. Her sex dripped its pungent discharge over the Queen's frantically rubbing hand. The Queen kept rubbing, past the panting girl's climax.

"Again, little slave girl," the Queen called to her, excitement in her voice. "Let it go! Come on! Again! Again!"

The French girl's eyes rolled back as she felt her pussy tremble and contract, pulsing against the hand that tormented her. Alliyah's eyes were wide with astonishment as she watched the grimace of passion on her face. Louder now, deep from within her throat, the enflamed girl moaned and groaned. "Uh! Uh! Uh! Uh! Uhhhhhhhh!" she cried out.

Satisfied, the Queen ceased her manipulations. The French girl's body sagged, causing her to lean against the Queen's shoulder. Slowly, her cries subsided.

"Oh, mother," the Princess whispered. "I never knew..."

"I know, sweetheart, I know," the Queen replied. "But now you do. That little flower between your legs can bring you much pleasure, my darling, and it takes a woman's touch to really bring it out. Men have no idea."

"What do you mean, mother?" the Princess asked, shocked by her mother's revelation.

"When she's been broken in, after the men have had their way with her, I'll bring her to you one night. She'll caress you like I just did to her, and she'll put her lips to your little flower and then you'll know what it means to be a woman."

"Oh, Mother, I, I..."

"Don't worry, my sweet. You're old enough now. You're to be married soon. You should know what pleasure your body can bring you before you spread your legs on the marriage bed."

The slave girl had recovered now from her orgasms. The Queen pulled her to her feet. The girl was dazed, overcome. She looked up at the stern, hard face of the Queen. She was grateful for the pleasure, but wary, fearful of what might come next.

"Ring for the guards," the Queen instructed the Princess. "We've got to get her cleaned up and ready for the party."

CHAPTER TEN

RUKIMO

All of the pathways of the resort were color-coded and the one to Rukimo's lair, as I learned to call it, was lined with broad black stripes laid horizontally across the concrete walkway. This denoted a security area, out of bounds to all but those with the highest clearance. The pathway snaked away from the resort area and led to a small bricked building. The entrance was guarded by two black robed security men, their robes as black as their skin. They wore black leather security belts from which hung long, tapered batons. There was a small case attached which contained a pair of handcuffs. The baton served as an instrument of discipline, as a blow from one would cause immediate, sharp pain. They also carried a small electric charge, with enough of a jolt to temporarily stun the most recalcitrant subject.

It did not happen often, but many of the men who habituated Klitzman's resort were tough, scabrous fellows. The resort was principally a paid-in club for men of wealth and power. Membership cost $500,000 a year, and visits were calculated at the rate of $10,000 per day. But it also served as a kind of R and R camp for many of Klitzman's felonious servants. These men ranged from the cold blooded killers so useful in the nether world of international crime, to the dealers, thieves and general racketeers that kept the flow of money and women flowing to and from this island. Sometimes these men had disputes. And sometimes the fiercely visaged security men had to step in and prevent violence. Any guest asked to leave Klitzman's resort due to misbehavior left it by way of a weighted body bag tossed off the end of a cabin cruiser.

The guards examined Anthony's pass and allowed us entrance. The outside door to the building led to a solitary room with an elevator. Since there was no second floor to the building, it only led one way: down.

The elevator rumbled to a halt and the shiny metal door slid open. We exited into a brightly lit corridor. The floor was covered with a thick red carpet and the cinderblock walls were painted white. A guard sat behind a large desk on which sat a series of television screens linked to security cameras mounted throughout the resort. Various scenes flickered on each of the screens, the combination of which constituted a sweep of the public areas of the resort.

The guard let us pass and we stopped by the first door on the left. Anthony pressed an intercom and the door buzzed open.

The room that we entered was a stark contrast to the institution-like ambiance of the hallway we had just left. It was a large, spacious room, wood paneled, a thick, oriental rug underfoot. A large, heavy desk dominated the room, dark oak, with ornate clubbed feet. Behind it sat a huge mass of a man, as black as coal, his neck thick and muscled. He was grinning widely as we entered.

"Harry Wiggins," he said in a deep, melodious voice, "I'm happy to make your acquaintance."

91

He rose from a plush leather chair and stepped around the desk. He wore a reddish brown robe like mine and Anthony's, but with bright red piping on its seams. He extended a meaty paw and fastened it on my hand with a vise-like grip. He stood at least a foot taller than me and his bulk blocked out all that was behind him.

"My pleasure, I'm sure," I responded, trying not to wince at the pressure on my hand.

"We have heard so much about you, Harry. I believe that you will fit in well around here."

"I hope so," I responded. I felt like I was at a Shriner's convention and I had just met the Grand Poobah.

"I've been waiting anxiously to meet you," Rukimo continued. "Let me order you some tea and we can sit and chat for a while."

The grizzly bear sized man pressed an intercom on his desk and spat out a command in what I took to be native African. A short noise of affirmation sounded back. Rukimo smiled and pointed to two large leather couches set in the corner of the room. In front of them was a large, square teak coffee table.

"Sit, Harry. We have much to discuss."

Anthony nodded at Rukimo and left the room. I was wary to be alone with the boss. Although no one had contacted me, and god knew if anyone ever would, I was still here under false pretenses. I had agreed to stool on Klitzman. If Rukimo had any inkling that I was bent, I would disappear forever in about three seconds flat.

As I sat on the couch, I took the opportunity to take

a closer look around Rukimo's private domain. Lining the wall opposite the couch where I sat was a series of six small cells, recessed into the wall. They were about three feet high and had heavy steel bars. Two of them were inhabited by naked, leather helmeted women. Their arms were fastened to leather belts around their waists. They were both on their knees, bent over, their bodies filling the small capacity of the cells.

In the corner of the room, arms locked behind her and dangling from a chain, was a frail looking, young Asian girl. She wore a leather gag in her mouth, but, unlike the women in the cages, her eyes were uncovered. She was standing on her toes, forced into that posture by the chain that pulled her arms up behind her. She had a forlorn, pained expression on her face. Her long, shiny black hair reached almost down to her waist, and framed her face as she held her head up to see what new demon had entered her life. I heard a muffled sob as she lowered her gaze to the floor, causing her hair to draw about her face like a shroud. I could see the evidence of a recent lashing on her inviting flesh, bright red stripes that crisscrossed her thighs.

"So, Harry," Rukimo began, "how was the trip?"

"Well, aside from the fine accommodations, it wasn't too bad."

"Oh," Rukimo laughed, a deep, hearty laugh, "you met Morianos. Not the most gracious of hosts. But he does a good day's work. These fine specimens, for example."

Rukimo motioned towards the two bound and caged women.

"You mean these are the broads that came on the plane with me?" I asked.

"Yes, yes," Rukimo answered. "We're going to have a little party with them shortly. I want to know more of why they were skulking around our little way station."

"Morianos said they were reporters."

"Perhaps," Rukimo replied. "On the other hand, being a reporter, or seeming to be one, is a good cover for other things. Our facility in the Venezuelan jungle is supposed to be secret. If these two could find it, then it may be time to shut it down."

Rukimo's speculation was interrupted by the entry of a black robed guard carrying a small tray. On it was a small teapot and two cups. He set them down before us wordlessly and then left.

Rukimo poured out two cups of the steaming tea. It was a dark, heavy blend, aromatic. It went down well.

"I'm sure you have questions, Harry," Rukimo continued. "Do you know why we selected you?"

"I supposed it had something to do with my skills with a .45," I answered.

"Ha, ha," Rukimo chuckled. "Yes, Harry. You proved your ruthlessness to us in the prison, but we knew of your reputation. Mr. Bianco spoke very highly of you."

So Tony had come through after all. "Maybe I could forget all about my deal with the Feds," I thought to myself.

"I don't suppose you have any jobs lined up for me yet, Mr. Rukimo," I said. Politeness was second nature in a world where people held the power of life or death over you.

"Just call me Rukimo, Harry. We don't stand on ceremony here. And no, we don't have anything lined up for you. For a while, you can relax and enjoy the amenities of our club. You've got a lot of time to make up for. Mr. Klitzman and I have a couple of ideas of where you can fit in to our operations, but we haven't come up with anything definite yet." Rukimo paused, taking a long sip of his tea.

It was weird to be sitting there, maybe twenty feet below ground, chit chatting like two genteel businessmen, sipping our tea, while three bound and naked women awaited our pleasure. I couldn't keep my eyes off of them while Rukimo spoke. My eyes darted over to the delicious flesh so often that Rukimo must have thought I had developed a tic. I was still lustful from the entertainment I had witnessed.

Rukimo continued his outline of my new role. "While you're here, Harry, you'll act as a supervisor. We want you to get used to dealing with our lifestyle. And I'll be frank, Harry, we want to know if you've got what it takes to deal with women as slaves. Once you go on the outside, you may get involved with some of our flesh peddling ventures and we can't afford to make any accommodation to the squeamish."

"Don't worry, Mr. Rukimo," I interjected. "I'll do whatever you want. I'm grateful for being sprung, and I know how to show gratitude."

"That's what I wanted to hear, Harry. Now, if you've finished your tea, you can come along and observe while we introduce these two slaves to their new lives."

Rukimo pressed an intercom button on a small table

next to the couch and barked out a command. A few moments later, two black robed guards entered the room. Rukimo and I rose as the guards unlocked the cages. The two women were dragged out and pulled to their feet. Two other guards entered the room pushing what looked like hand trucks. I could hear muffled squeals from the women as they were manhandled by the guards. Their bodies sagged as their knees, cramped for who knew how long, failed to support them. The two women were quickly mounted on the hand trucks, their bodies belted in. A belt that ran under their arms and just above their breasts held them in a standing position. Rukimo and I followed as the women were wheeled from the room.

We went down the red carpeted hallway to a locked steel door. The door was opened after the pressing of a buzzer, by a guard on the other side. The door led to another long hallway. Cells lined the hallway, small ten by ten cells. Most of them were occupied by naked, leather helmeted women, either shackled to a cot or dangling from a chain affixed to the ceiling. I counted ten cells on each side.

"These are all slaves in training," Rukimo explained as we walked down the hall. "This is a rest period. The ones standing are being punished. Try standing stretched out on your toes for a couple of hours. It's a most effective torture."

"I'll bet," I said. From what I could see, all of the women were delightful in form. Their faces were obscured by the hoods that they wore, but their other charms were plain to see.

"The hoods not only block out all light," Rukimo

continued as we proceeded down the hall, "but they block out all sound too. There are small battery powered speakers near the ears that transmit a stream of static. This way, the subjects are kept in total isolation when not actively training. It helps demonstrate their total helplessness and vulnerability. And the sensory deprivation makes them more malleable."

It wasn't hard to imagine what fear and desperation could be inculcated in a young helpless victim by cutting them off from almost all sensation. I was beginning to understand why Rukimo wanted to be assured that his employees harbored no sentimentality.

We reached the end of the hallway and entered a large dimly lit room. It had a dais in the middle, elevated from the floor be a couple of feet. The hand trucks were brought vertical and the women presented for view. I wondered how long these two had been held in isolation. I guessed that it was, for the most part, ever since they had arrived. Their minds had to be rife with confusion and fear.

Rukimo paused before the two displayed women. He turned to me. "Well, Harry, who should we start with?"

It was hard to tell which one was which. The hoods deprived the women of all personality. From what I remembered, the one who had hung by her wrists all night when I was at Morianos' had been a little taller, more developed. But the women were slumped in their confinements so that was not much help. But it really didn't matter which one I picked. I knew that this was my first test from Rukimo. I was being asked which of the two women would be the first to be subjected to a tortuous interrogation. If I flinched at choosing, Rukimo would begin to have doubts as to my suitability for his uses. I pointed to the one at my left.

Rukimo nodded to the guards and the woman who I had selected was loosened from her confinements and dragged up to the dais. Her hands were released from the belt and attached to a chain that hung from the ceiling. The chain was shortened by the operation of a winch and shortly the woman was dangling on her toes.

There were several easy chairs spread across the room and two were brought over to the front of the dais. Rukimo sat in one and motioned me to sit in the other. The second woman was released from her hand truck and brought over to Rukimo. I could see that she was trembling. After such a long period of time confined and inactive, the suddenness of her transport from Rukimo's office to here had to be a disconcerting experience. The woman's breasts swayed gently as she was presented to Rukimo. Long brown hair descended from the leather helmet. Her hands strained at the belt that circled her waist. Sweat glistened on her chest, the product of her fear. She was right to be afraid.

Rukimo pulled the woman onto his lap. Her pale flesh was a stark contrast to his black skin. His right hand ran over her breasts and then between her legs. She still wore her brown bush. One of the guards unlocked the hood and pulled it from her head. It was the reporter, the one Morianos had fucked and abused. Her hair was matted from its confinement in the leather hood. Her face was flush, her eyes wild with terror. The gag was still in her mouth. She looked up at her friend, hooded, naked and suspended by her arms.

She took in the faces of the large black guards in the room, remorseless, frightening faces. They all seemed to be anticipating the next developments with relish. When the reporter turned her head to see on whose lap she sat, she grimaced. Rukimo was smiling at her, a determined, cruel smile.

"Welcome to Africa," he intoned. "I'm delighted to make your acquaintance."

The girl's eyes began to tear. She knew from Rukimo's smiling face and his solid grip on her body that something terrible was going to happen to her very soon.

"I believe that you've met my friend Harry," Rukimo teased. His left arm was around her waist, holding her still on his lap. The girl looked at me briefly. Her eyes were glistening with tears, her face ashen. I could see the goose bumps on her tender, soft skin. Her nipples were stiff. The beauteous orbs on her chest rocked gently as she struggled to calm her panicked breath.

The girl's attention was drawn back to her captor as Rukimo's right hand stroked the inside of her thighs. "You and I are going to have a little chat, darling. But first, we have a little entertainment. Your friend is going to do a little dance for us."

Rukimo motioned to one of the guards who stepped up on the dais. He held a long, leather encased cane. It didn't take a genius to figure out what he was going to do with it.

The girl on Rukimo's lap began to whine and struggle. Rukimo had buried his hand between her thighs and he must have squeezed her pussy lips hard because she stiffened and moaned. Rukimo spoke to her softly.

"My dear, you mustn't squirm. It's very distracting. Besides, I want you to enjoy the show."

Rukimo nodded to the guard holding the cane. The heavyset, well-muscled guard reared his arm back and struck the dangling woman across her back. There was a loud 'crack!' and a muffled moan escaped from the woman's gag. Her whole body cringed, as the pain from the unexpected blow reverberated through her. Another and another blow fell across her back. Each kiss of the cane on the poor woman's body permeated the otherwise silent room with the unmistakable sound of leather striking flesh.

All eyes were on the spectacle unfolding on the dais. The guards were uniformly grinning as they took in the steady pummeling of the tormented woman. Even the girl on Rukimo's lap was transfixed by what she saw.

The whipping of the helpless naked and hooded woman continued unmercifully. She squirmed and danced as each blow fell. A high pitched wail could be heard emanating from her gag. The guard handling the whip had crossed to the woman's front, and I could see bright lines of red rise immediately on the tortured flesh as he began to torment her breasts, belly and thighs. The girl was screaming loudly behind her gag while she twisted and turned in futile attempts to avoid the cane's painful bite.

I had never witnessed a whipping. I had seen men beaten, I had seen women slapped around, but the steady, remorseless application of pain to a woman's body was novel to me. There was something strangely exciting about watching the tender flesh writhe and twist in response to the blows. The woman's breasts jerked wildly about, forced into incessant motion by her desperate movements. Sweat dripped from her body, making it glisten. The muted groans and screams of pain sent chills up and down my spine. I could feel my cock hardening as the clear message of physical dominance of the whipped woman was brought home to me. Soon, I knew, she would be opened for the pleasure of the men in the room. No one would ask her permission.

I looked over at the woman on Rukimo's lap. Her face was a picture of horror as she witnessed the abuse of her friend. Tears flowed down her cheeks. She had to know that what she was witnessing was her own future, her own fate. Soon, she would face the same or a similar ordeal. From where I sat, I could see that she was ready to do anything to avoid it.

The whipping of the woman on the dais finally stopped. She hung seemingly lifeless in her chains. Only her low moans gave evidence that she retained consciousness. Her body was crisscrossed with welts. She had suffered a terrible beating and, because of the hood, which blocked out all sight and sound, she had no idea why or by whom she was being tortured.

Two of the guards went over to the side of the room where I saw a small brazier that had been apparently lit before we came in. The coals were beginning to gleam red. Two bars of iron sat in the fire, their ends buried in the searing heat. I speculated on their prospective use and I recalled the scarred 'K' I had seen on the slave Adriana this morning. I expected that I would see the same mark on the two women before us ere long.

The girl on Rukimo's lap was sobbing. Her whole body heaved with panic and fear. Rukimo's jet black hand was crammed between her thighs. His other hand was massaging a breast. The girl's breasts were large and bulbous, yet seemed small compared to Rukimo's massive mitt. Her flesh was white, tender, a sharp contrast to the dark and rough hand that had captured it.

Rukimo spoke to the girl softly, "Well, darling, have you ever seen anything like that? Would you like to take your turn?"

The girl's eyes pleaded to be spared the other girl's ordeal. A small whine escaped her gag. Her nipples, surrounded by large, dark areolae, were stiff with fear. She shook he head desperately. More tears cascaded down her face.

"Well," Rukimo continued, "let's have a little chat and we'll see what happens. O.K.?" The girl nodded desperately.

Pushing the girl's head down, Rukimo used both his hands to unfasten the leather straps that held the gag into her mouth. He pulled her head back and placed his hand on the outside of the gag. He looked her in the eyes.

"Now, we must be quiet, darling. No outbursts, please. And you must answer all of my questions, do you understand?"

The girl, her brow furrowed with worry, nodded again. Rukimo pulled the long, thick leather gag from her mouth.

I could see the girl's trembling lips as she exercised

her jaw, finally free from its brutal extension by the gag. She was no teenager, probably about 25 or 26. But her relative maturity had surely not prepared her for what she had just witnessed. She could have never guessed that one day she would be held a naked, bound prisoner in an unknown land and at the mercy of harsh, unscrupulous men. She was probably very brave. She and her friend had risked doom by spying on Klitzman's operations. That took nerve. But two days of sensory deprivation, being flown thousands of miles to an unknown destination, kept naked and confined for many hours, had certainly eroded her inner strength. And now she had witnessed the callous, casual beating of her friend. She could be forgiven for quaking in fear.

Rukimo elbowed her legs wider apart and I could see that he had his fingers jammed into her sex. Whether the product of fear, or of Rukimo's manipulation of her flesh, I did not know, but Rukimo's fingers were glistening with her moisture. He moved his stocky black fingers in and out of the pinkish hole with ease. I could see the nascent signs of physical excitement on her chest, red blotches rising on her alabaster skin.

Rukimo started to interrogate the girl.

"Now, darling, tell me your name."

The girl looked taken aback at the direct question and the opportunity to speak. The words were difficult for her to get out. Her voice was faint, almost indiscernible.

"M-my name is Lois G-Gardner," the girl replied unsteadily.

"Well, Lois Gardner, are you what you pretend to

be? We have your identification. It says that you are a reporter for the New York Gazette. Is this true?"

"Yes," the girl squeaked in reply.

"Well we have checked and we could find no record of a Lois Gardner on the staff of the New York Gazette. Are you sure that you want to keep that story?"

"It's true, it's true," the girl blurted out. "I'm a free-lancer. They gave me credentials so that I could get some cooperation from the American Embassy and the Venezuelan Government." Her voice was desperate. She had to realize that if Rukimo believed she was lying that she would soon take a turn on the dais.

Rukimo kept up a relentless questioning of the girl. What was the name of her editor? What magazines had she written for in the past? Where did she live? Where did she go to school? These were all questions designed to blow her cover if she was indeed more than she seemed to be. If the information was false, it could be easily checked. And it would be hard to get all the details of a cover story right under the duress the frightened girl was subject to in this dimly lit dungeon.

The questioning shifted to the other girl. Her name was Delia Fremont. She was a photographer. They had met only days before their trip to South America. No, they were not lovers. Lois didn't know much about her except she said that she was from the Midwest. Delia was the one with the local contacts. Delia had proposed going into the jungle to find the landing zone. Delia had gotten the Jeep. Delia had gotten the directions.

Lois's voice grew somewhat calmer now as she recovered her sense of speech. I could detect a slight pant to her breath. Rukimo had continued to manipulate her pussy throughout the interrogation and its effects were telling. Lois took advantage of a pause to try and close her thighs. Rukimo responded instantly by twisting and turning the lips to her sex. Lois moaned in pain.

"Don't try and hide your pretty little cunt, Lois," Rukimo taunted her. "Everyone wants to see it. I think Harry here wants to fuck it. Don't you Harry?"

I felt a lump in my throat. It wasn't from fear, it was from unbridled passion. I had never felt so hot for a fuck as I did now.

"Sure," was all that I managed to eke out.

"See, darling Lois, you're going to have to please Harry soon. And my other friends too. I just want to get you good and wet so that their cocks will go in nice and easy."

Lois was cringing as Rukimo's words sank into her. She was going to be gang banged and there was no power in the world that was going to stop it. She began to plead with Rukimo.

"Oh, please don't do this, please. My newspaper will pay you. I won't say anything about what I saw. Please," she begged piteously.

"My darling, you are never going back to New York," Rukimo answered her. "We want you here. You are now the property of Mr. Klitzman. He wants you to learn to be a good little whore. And I think your lesson should begin now."

The pitiful creature looked forlornly around the room for help. All she saw were the lustful eyes of Rukimo's crew. And me. I too lusted after this unhappy girl. My cock was hard with desire. Anthony had been right. Prison was never like this.

Rukimo grabbed Lois's face with his broad, gnarly hand. He squeezed her cheeks harshly. She whimpered in pain.

"You are going to get down on your knees, slave, and you are going to suck my cock," he told her. "When you are done, we will have a little surprise for you. If you don't do a good job, you will take your friend's place on the dais."

Lois nodded her head, denoting her submission to Rukimo's demand. He pushed her off of his lap and opened his robe. His thick, black cock was at high attention. Lois sank to her knees, tears cascading down her face. She looked up at Rukimo's implacable eyes. There was no pity there. Only cruelty. Slowly, she bent at the waist, shuffled forwards on her knees and engulfed the sleek head of Rukimo's tool between her trembling lips.

The whiteness of Lois's skin made Rukimo's seem all the darker. Her head bobbed up and down rapidly as if she wanted to hasten the end of her ordeal. I had a side view of her face and I could see her lips distend and contract as she ran them up and down Rukimo's ebony manhood. But Rukimo had no desire to abbreviate his enjoyment of Lois's mouth. He grabbed her head with his hands and pressed her down on his cock, forcing it into her throat. I could hear the abject woman gag and choke. As she struggled for air Rukimo leaned over and spoke softly into her ear.

"Now, my dear, I want you to take your time on my cock. Feel its strength with your tongue. We have all day to play. Make me believe you enjoy it."

He released the pressure on Lois's head and she came up for air. He allowed her two quick gulps and he pressed her head back to its task. Now she had the rhythm Rukimo wanted. Slowly, she rose and fell. Rukimo leaned back in the chair, his eyes closed, letting the pleasurable sensations flow through him. For a good ten minutes, Lois worked Rukimo's rod. Her breasts jiggled tantalizingly as she made her best efforts to please her captor. Rukimo opened his eyes and looked at me.

"Would you like to fuck her, Harry?" he asked. "Get behind her and fill her pussy with your meat. I'll bet it's nice and tight."

He didn't have to ask me twice. I loosened my robe and fell behind the girl. Her legs were pressed together and I had to spread them wider with my hands. Her thighs were sweaty and hot. I reached between her legs and felt her pussy from behind. It was still wet from Rukimo's ministrations. I pressed my fingers inside, distending the lips. I could smell her involuntary arousal. Its pungent odor enflamed my passion. I pressed my hot piece against her loins and thrust forwards. I slid right in.

Lois began to whimper again as she suffered another unwanted violation of her body. But I paid her muffled protests no mind as the wet warmth of her channel triggered a wave of pleasure in my brain. I began to thrust, at first slowly, but soon, my lust began to over whelm me and I pumped harder and faster.

Rukimo laughed. "Let me know when you're going to come, Harry. We'll fill her with our spunk from both ends at once."

I grunted in reply. It did not take long and I felt the telltale tingling in my balls. All of my consciousness was focused on my prick as it began to throb. "I'm going to come," I shouted. "I'm coming!"

Pulse after pulse of pleasure shot through me as I emptied my balls into her womb. I could hear Rukimo's grunts and the protesting whinny of the girl, evidencing Rukimo's delivery of a load of hot sperm into her mouth. She shuddered and rocked against me. Her passion had risen too and I could feel her contractions with my cock as she orgasmed. She didn't need to be trained as a whore, she already was one.

I slowly recovered from my explosion of lust. I rubbed my hands across the fine white globes of the girl's rear. They were soft and hot, fleshy, but yet hard. She was a fine piece all right. My softened cock popped out of her loins and I pulled myself to my feet. Rukimo was busy wiping his cock's last drops of cum over Lois's face. She was still whimpering.

"A good blow job, Lois, I can see you've had some experience. You'll fit in well here," Rukimo said to the girl tauntingly. "There's just one more piece of business and then I'm going to leave you to the pleasures of my friends."

Rukimo snapped his fingers. The guards, who had been watching Lois's initiation into her new life with undisguised lust, sprang into action. One guard stepped up on the dais and locked his legs around the legs of Delia, who was still dangling from her chains, oblivious to the rape of her friend. Another guard came from behind Delia carrying a long rod with a red hot tip.

Pulling Lois to her feet by her hair, Rukimo directed her attention to the other woman.

"Now, dear Lois," he said in his deep, gruff musically accented voice, "now that your friend and you have become Mr. Klitzman's property, you need to be marked appropriately. This way if you get lost or run away, people will know where to bring you back. I want you to take a good look, because your turn will come next."

Lois looked up and saw the tall, broad shouldered African holding what could be nothing other than a branding iron. He smiled at her, his bright white teeth gleaming. Lois could not believe her eyes. "Oh, god, no!" she cried out. "Oh, god, please don't do this, please! Oh, no, no, no!" She was trembling as Rukimo held her head still, directed at the tableau on the dais. Her knees must have buckled because her body sagged. But Rukimo's grip kept her standing, forced to witness the barbarous act that was about to be performed.

"Cattle," I thought. "They brand cattle." Were these women to be no more than two footed cattle? Were all the female prisoners here no more than livestock, pretty, compliant, pleasurable animals? Apparently that was what they were, and what Lois and Delia were about to become.

Now Delia, of course, had no inkling of the cruel indignity she was about to experience. She must have been confused when the guard's body pressed up against hers. Was she about to be raped? Was she to feel the bite of the lash once again? He was holding her body immobile, his black limbs entwined with her white ones. Her helmeted head bobbed nervously over the shoulder of her assailant. Suddenly, the guard with the branding iron stepped forward. Lois shrieked as the flaming red end, the bright, cursive "k", was pressed into Delia's rear. There was a sizzling sound and a distinct odor of burning flesh.

It was hard to believe that anyone so thoroughly gagged could make as much noise as emanated from Delia. Although muffled, her scream of pain tore through the room as the shocking pain coursed through her body. Her torso seemed to jump in place. The guard who held her struggled to keep her still. The brand burned into her flesh for a full three seconds, seconds that I was sure felt like an eternity to the tortured woman. What could she be thinking, deprived of all sight and sound for so long? Processes were at work on her that she could not control. The terrible sting of the brand was but a harbinger of what was to come. She was being turned into an object, an unperson.

Lois's shrieks had subsided into blubbering tears. One of the guards released Delia from her chains. The abused woman fell into the other guard's arms. He quickly drew her off of the stage. Another guard took Lois by the arm. It was her turn.

Lois realized at once what was afoot. She vainly tried to pull away from the guard, but he had her arms firmly in his hands. He easily pulled her up onto the dais. She had gone limp and her feet dragged along the floor. As she was brought to the dangling chain, she began to beg and cry. "Please don't brand me, oh, please!" she cried forlornly. "I'll do anything you say, I'll do anything! Please! Please!"

One guard held her up by her hair as the other unlocked her hands from behind her. She was twisting and turning frantically, flailing her hands and arms about. The brawny guard easily captured first one arm, and then the other, and affixed them to the bracelets that hung on the end of the chain. The woman's face was a grotesque grimace as she desperately struggled with her captors. She swung a foot out at one of the guards, which he sidestepped easily. The other responded by a sharp jab to Lois's stomach. She gasped in surprise and pain.

The blow to Lois's stomach ended her resistance. The chain was pulled higher so as to extend her body until just her toes touched the floor. She was drawing deep breaths, struggling for air as a result of the blow to her midsection. Everyone stood still while she regained her breath.

When she had recovered, Lois looked forlornly around the room. "Was this really going to happen?" her expression seemed to say. She met only cold, stone hard faces.

Rukimo signaled to the guard by the brazier who brought another red tipped branding iron up to the dais. The air was still pungent with the scent of Delia's burnt flesh. She was still moaning as she lay where she had been dropped to the floor, her hands reaffixed behind her back. A long, pitiful whine escaped Lois's lips as she saw the branding iron brought forth. She looked over to Rukimo, her eyes imploring, tears running down her cheeks.

"Why are you doing this?" she asked him.

Rukimo rose to his full height. All playfulness was

out of his voice now. He radiated power and cruelty.

"We're going this, Ms. Gardner, or should I say soon to be the former Ms. Gardner, because you're a nosy cunt. Nosy cunts get disposed of, Ms. Gardner. Just be thankful that you and your friend are young and desirable enough to be kept here as slaves. Because the alternative would be a little swim with the sharks in Limpala Bay. I invite you to scream your loudest, Ms. Gardner, it will be the last sound you make as a human being."

Quickly, a guard stepped in front of the distended woman and wrapped his body around hers. I could see her face poking up over the blacked robed figure. Her eyes were scrunched closed, her face distorted in fear. The other guard stepped forward.

The former Ms. Gardner's scream was the loudest sound that I have ever heard a human being make. It pierced my ears painfully. She drowned out the sound of her flesh being scorched, but the scent of burned meat soured the room. Her bladder must have loosened from the shock as urine poured from her sex down onto the rug. As she strained to catch her breath after her piteous scream, I could hear the water dripping on the rug, an almost comical diversion from her certainly anything but comical pain.

The girl, mercifully, fainted. She dangled loosely in the chains. A guard laughed and said something to Rukimo in their native dialect. Rukimo and the other guards joined in the merriment. I was too stunned to wonder what he had said. It must take a cruelly depraved mind to find humor in the reporter's and her friend's fates, I thought. Rukimo looked over at me. I tried to look unaffected by the torture I had just witnessed.

"So Harry, ever see anything like that in Atlantic City?" Rukimo asked me.

"I can't say that I did," I answered.

The guards were busy draping the bodies of Lois and Delia over two waist high stanchions. Their arms and legs were spread and lashed to the wooden frames. I sensed that their torment was to continue.

Rukimo slapped one of the guards on the back and then walked over to me. "Now the boys will have their fun. Let's go back to my office and talk about your new duties."

I acquiesced in Rukimo's command. As we left the room, I turned for a last look at the two females. Lois had been rehooded and both she and Delia had a guard poised behind them, between their outstretched legs, thick black cocks hardening in their hands.

CHAPTER ELEVEN

A SLAVE GIRL MEETS HER MASTER

After she was rehooded and trundled away, the French girl was brought to the slave quarters of the Palace. The Emirate was a small country and the Emir was minor royalty, and so his palace was not quite as lavish as one might think. His current staff consisted of seven slave girls, three wives, fifteen children, his mother, three mothers-in-law, four dogs, eight cats, five horses and a Maserati. There was a small cooking staff, a cleaning staff and a serving staff.

There was also one particular individual whose job it was to regulate and control the slave staff. He was a tall, light brown muscular African, with shaved head and a deficit of gonads. The slave girls all feared him, for it was he who maintained their discipline, punishing them for infractions, keeping them ready, willing and able to serve the Emir or his guests. Lately, the Emir's eldest son, Rashan, the Prince, had taken to enjoying himself with his father's owned flesh, and it was the African who brought pain and suffering upon them when the Prince was not satisfied with their enthusiastic service of his lusts.

It was the slavemaster, Ngomo, whose face the French Girl next saw when her hood was removed. She knew at once that this would be the new true power in her life. She had seen the faces of callous men before, men who tokened no disobedience, who demanded precise compliance with orders, who took delight in the administration of the lash. This man was clearly one of those. He was dressed in his standard uniform, a long, white dashiki that flowed down to his thick leather sandals. His face was boney and hard, his eyes, sunk deep beneath his brow, were black as death. The girl trembled before him.

Ngomo grabbed the girl by her hair and pulled her erect. He perused her charms with disdain. He spun her around and bent her over to look at her ass and to probe from behind her still lubricated loins. The girl was bent over, almost in half, and she could see the gnarled hand of the overseer as it familiarized itself with her cleft. She saw the hand press her labial lips together and squeeze them harshly. Too afraid to struggle, the slave girl whined in pain and humiliation. The guards who had brought her to Ngomo still were standing around and she could hear them exchange witty comments about the new slut. The pain continued in her loins and she moaned loudly, the leather ball in her mouth stifling the full effect of her exclamations. Ngomo took hold of her clit and he was twisting and turning it, pinching it painfully.

The slave was being taught her first lesson. Ngomo ruled in the slave quarters. She would obey him, his rules or suffer.

Her head finally released, her loins freed of the harsh grasp of Ngomo, the French girl raised her torso hesitatingly. She kept her teary eyes downcast as she sought to communicate her deference to this cruel man, her understanding of his message. Ngomo shooed the guards away and, grabbing the girl's left nipple, led her into the harem. Only he and the Emir had keys. He paused to unlock the steel gate that barred its entrance and pulled the girl in behind him.

The gates led to a large foyer with a shiny green marble floor. Tall white columns held up a broad, circular canopy. Without ado, Ngomo dragged the girl further into the harem proper. They descended a small set of stairs that led to a large, luxuriously decorated room, filled with large, overstuffed cushions of maroon leather, small tables of deep mahogany. There were large, heavily braided pillows decorated with deep reds and carmine flourishes. Spread liberally about the room were scantily clad young females, lounging here and there, talking quietly to each other, brushing each other's hair. They all looked up when Ngomo entered the room and, as one, ceased their former activities and knelt on the floor, their foreheads pressed to the deep piled, plush oriental rug, their hands pressed palms up behind their backs.

Ngomo stood tall, and in a deep, resonating voice issued his orders to the abject females.

"This is the Master's new slave. You will call her Fatima. She is to be bathed, perfumed and decorated within the hour. You will have two weeks to teach her what she needs to know and to understand commands. If she does not learn all of this within two weeks, you will all be punished harshly."

With that, Ngomo released the French girl, now officially called Fatima, and strode from the room.

Slowly, the seven curvaceous and obedient beauties rose from the floor. They all cast their eyes on their new sister. Some looked with disdain and dislike, jealous of their ranking in the slave hierarchy. Some looked with compassion, remembering their first frightened, disoriented day in the Emir's harem. And some looked on her with fear, knowing the difficulty of the task ahead of teaching this unknown female what she had to learn to survive, knowing all too well the dire consequences of failure.

The first to approach Fatima was a yellow haired beauty named Gelela, not her 'real' name, of course, but the name issued to her by her master, just like the short, white laced, baby doll nightclothes that she wore. It was more revealing than not, as the tips of her taut, round breasts poked through the gaps in the lace. The garment reached only just below her sex and so the least movement revealed the delightful lips between her thighs. It was, with minor variations, the standard dress for the harem. Some of the girl's wore sheer, silk chemises, either black or a deep red. Others wore laced garments like Gelela's, but of different shades and hues.

Gelela was an American by birth. She did not know exactly how long she had been a guest of the Emir, or how long it was since she last tasted free air. She tried not to think about that anymore. She was a slave and it was a slave's fate that would be hers.

The American stepped up to Fatima and solicitously placed her soft hand on the younger girl's delicate cheek. Her eyes softened, communicating wordlessly to Fatima her empathy with her plight. She saw the leather ball wedged into the French girl's mouth and tenderly began to remove it.

"No, don't!" cried a slender, red headed girl by her

side. She wore a red silk nightgown, sheer and short. Her breasts were larger than the American's, her hair longer. She was British, and spoke in well refined, rounded tones. "He didn't say to remove the gag!" she said urgently. "Do you want to get us all thrashed!"

Gelela halted her hand. English was the lingua franca of the harem. The girls were purposely kept as ignorant of Arabic as possible. Any direct communication with them by the Emir or his guests was short and to the point. No one wanted to know what they thought, or felt the need to convey their innermost yearnings to them. They were there to fuck, be pretty, and scream and moan nicely when beaten.

The French girl's English was mostly limited to what she had learned in her training and service at Klitzman's resort. She did not know what the two dolorously clad women before her were saying. She knew what the big coffee colored man had said pertained to her, and she heard the menace in his voice. But that was all.

The other girls had crowded around their new companion. A tall, black haired girl, with long, lanky legs and bright green eyes pushed Gelela aside. She was top dog here. She had been quite the athlete before she had been whisked off a Madrid street one day shortly after her twenty-first birthday. Three years of life as a slave had toughened her. She knew how to cause pain in ways that didn't show, and all of the others had witnessed or experienced her ire at one time or another.

"Let's get a look at the new cunt," she said, harshly. Gelela and the redhead gave way to her. She stood before the newly christened Fatima and took in the slender hips, the small, but gracefully formed breasts. She knew competition when she saw it. This one would have to be taught right away who was first in the harem.

"Do you speak English, cunt," she asked Fatima as she grabbed the girl's chin and pushed her head upwards. Fatima looked back wordlessly. "Well," the Spanish beauty continued, "whether you do or not, I'll bet you understand this." The Spanish girl reared back and smote Fatima a solid blow to her midsection. The girl collapsed, her breath taken away, a deep, aching hollowness forming in her stomach. As the Spanish girl walked away, Gelela and the redhead stood back in shock. All the girls remained silent. The only sound was the desperate gasping of the French girl as she knelt on the floor, her bound hands twisting behind her.

Gelela recovered first and she bent down to aid the stricken new girl. The redhead, whose name was Jamilah, knelt beside her, and together they brought the French girl to her feet. The girl cringed and moaned, fearful of a resumed assault. By gentle stroking and soft cooing, the two women gradually calmed her. The other women had disbursed, going back to their monotonous routines. A small television in the corner of the room showed American soap operas and today they would find out whether Paul was sleeping with Vicki and whether Rosemarie would survive her surgery.

Gelela and Jamilah gently escorted Fatima from the common room to the sleeping quarters. There was a large bathroom near the entrance and Fatima allowed herself to be escorted inside. Gelela began to run a bath in the sumptuous, oversized sunken tub. There was enough room in the tub for several of the women to bathe at once, and often the girls would languish in it, hot oily water refreshing their skin.

The French girl had calmed now, as she understood what was going to happen. She looked forwards to a bath, removing the sweat and stink of her close confinement, relaxing in fragrant waters. Slaves took pleasure where they could.

Fatima fully expected to have her hands unlocked so that she could bath. But she was wrong.

"Do you think we should undo her hands," Gelela asked the redhead.

"I'm not doing anything that I haven't been told to do," Jamilah answered. "If Ngomo wanted her hands unfastened, he would have done it. Besides," she said looking behind the French girl's back at the bracelets that confined her wrists, "we don't have the key."

One of the other girls, a young Asian woman, a mere wisp of a girl, entered the bathroom. Her black hair was short and straight and her small breasts made tiny bumps under the beige, silk, crotchless teddy that she wore. Her lower lips were shaved and sported a large ring. She was a recent arrival, a gift to the Emir from a Japanese consortium looking to win a construction contract. The American Navy was coming and there was going to be plenty of money floating around for a long time. The Emir anticipated many such gifts in the near future.

The Asian girl's English was coming along, but she tended to talk in clipped sentences. Her voice was demure, high pitched. "May I help?" she asked timidly. She too had experienced a similar greeting from the Spaniard when she arrived.

"Oh, thank you Me Ling," Gelela answered. "Keep her calm while I get a sponge and some soap."

Me Ling quickly shed her garment and stepped into the rising water. She was at least a head shorter than the French girl, her figure almost boyish. "Come, come," she called to her.

The confused French girl stepped forwards gingerly. It appeared that she was not to be given the freedom to wash herself. As she stepped into the steaming water, the soothing heat spread up her legs. She moaned slightly.

"Yes, yes," Me Ling called to her. She tenderly pulled on Fatima's elbow and urged her into the vast pool like tub.

The redheaded Jamilah had also disrobed and she joined the other women in the tub. Gelela, returning with a large, soft sponge and a squeeze bottle of scented soap, handed them off to Jamilah and, after removing her delicate babydoll, stepped in.

The three harem slaves admired the fine curves and delicate contours of the French girl's body. Gelela ran her hand over Fatima's rear and discovered the indentation of her brand. "Oh, look," she said to the other girls. They knew the meaning of the red, cursive 'K'. Gelela turned her back to the French girl and pointed to a matching inscription burned into her body. Jamilah did the same. Fatima looked back with understanding.

Not all of the slaves had made their way to the

Emir's harem by way of Klitzman's island. Gelela and Jamilah had, Me Ling and a few of the others had not. All told, four of the seven slaves were graduates of Klitzman's special resort. With Fatima, that made five.

Gelela motioned Fatima to crouch down in the water. As Fatima lowered herself obediently, the other three women joined her.

The hot water was soothing to Fatima. The three girls gently crowded around her, their kind eyes seeking hers, their soft hands rubbing her back and arms. The French girl sighed softly and began to cry. There was no kindness at Klitzman's island. There had been no delicate, soothing caresses. Life had been hard and cruel. The girl had penned up all of her sorrow, all of her fear, all of her yearnings for peace. And now, as her chest heaved with hearty sobs, she let it all out.

The three other women circled her with their arms. For several minutes the women sat, conjoined, memories of love and happiness revived by Fatima's piteous wails. Tears were flowing all around. After a short while, wiping her now reddened eyes, Gelela brushed Fatima's cheek softly with her hand, clearing away a lock of frizzled hair, and planted her lips directly on the girl's trembling lips. Fatima, desperately thankful for the show of kindness and understanding she had been shown, yearning to reciprocate Gelela's affection, opened her lips and absorbed the blonde girl's gently probing tongue. Me Ling had daringly removed the heavy leather ball that had deprived Fatima of speech since her arrival, and Gelela was free to explore the French girl's greedy mouth. A hand pressed against the girl's breast, cupping and caressing the soft orb.

Hands spread her thighs.

The pool had a sloped end, where the girl's could lie down and keep their heads above water. As of one mind, the three harem girls pulled Fatima towards it and pushed her back. Me Ling sat behind her to ease the strain on her bound wrists, receiving her graceful, round shoulders into her lap. Hands drew Fatima's legs apart. A mouth fastened on her breast. Gelela's tongue danced slowly in her mouth. The French girl groaned lustfully. Never since her rude awakening deep in Klitzman's dungeon had the girl felt the warmth of loving lips, the caress of caring hands. As her place of pleasure was gently stroked below the warm, comforting water, she sensed her orgasm rising inside her. For the first time in many months, she yearned for it, welcomed it, not as a drug, a moment of passionate release from her nightmare, but as a gift to her new found lovers, the three women who were giving her the gift of themselves.

When she came it was like wave of deliverance washing over her. She moaned into Gelela's mouth. The mouth on her breast sucked harder on her teat, giving an almost painful edge to her orgasm. And then, the forceful throbbing in her loins subsided. The three women, sensing the end to her release, calmed their ministrations. Two sets of arms held her tight while Me Ling softly stroked her head, murmuring in her native tongue sweet words of love.

The women lay entwined for a few moments more when Gelela came alert with a start. They had to get the new girl ready or they would all be whipped to an inch of their lives.

"Come on," she said to the others, "we've got to get moving."

The three women pulled Fatima to her feet and began to sponge her body. Me Ling moved to return the leather ball to Fatima's mouth. As she did so, Fatima looked into her eyes, tears forming at the edges and whispered, "Merci," in a low, soft voice.

Me Ling kissed her lightly on the lips and restored the leather ball to her mouth.

Fifteen minutes later, Fatima sat on a stool before a mirror. Me Ling was drying and combing out her hair. Gelela was carefully painting the tips of her breasts. Jamilah watched at the doorway for any sign of Ngomo.

Me Ling finished with Fatima's hair after combing in a light, perfumed oil. Gelela had painted Fatima's nipples a dark red and then spread her legs to adorn her nether lips. Jamilah was the expert at facial adornment and so switched places with Gelela. She hurriedly, but expertly, outlined Fatima's lips with the bright red lipstick Gelela had used on her nipples and outer labia. She worked a line of black around the edges of her eyes and curled her lashes. She applied a dark blush to her cheeks, just enough to highlight the deep red of her lips.

Me Ling, meanwhile undertook the task of painting Fatima's fingernails. It was a difficult undertaking since Fatima's wrists were still conjoined. By the time Jamilah was finished with Fatima's face, she had started on the toes. When she was finished, the women pulled Fatima from her stool and sprayed her with a light scent of jasmine, applying the spray to her breasts and her loins.

Jamilah stood before the newly decorated girl and admired their handiwork. "Oh, you're beautiful Fatima. I could eat you up."

Gelela turned and hissed, "Ngomo!"

They had finished just in time. Woe betides them if they hadn't done a good job.

Ngomo strode into the bathroom. Then three slaves fell to their knees and bowed to their taskmaster. Fatima was at a loss of what to do. Ngomo stepped up to her and examined her with a well trained eye. He held her cheeks with one hand and turned her head right and left to judge the quality of the slaves' handiwork. He seemed satisfied.

Fatima was still wearing the leather cuffs and steel collar that had adorned her when she had been shipped from Klitzman's island. The Emir's slaves did not wear cuffs or ankle restraints. When necessary to immobilize them a length of leather thong was used or a set of steel bracelets that seemed to be always at hand. But they did wear collars, narrow, gleaming, golden collars with rings affixed fore and aft. A small disk hung from the ring in the front containing the Emir's crest on one side and the name of the slave engraved on the other.

"Follow me," Ngomo ordered. Fatima's English was rudimentary, but this order she understood. Her hands still bound behind her, she scurried after Ngomo as he strode from the bathroom. Once in the common area, he had her stand still while he removed the restraints from her wrists and ankles. It felt strange to Fatima to have her hands free after so long a confinement. He then turned her around and removed the steel collar. A delicate golden one took its place.

The three women who had been grooming Fatima ran out of the bedroom with a selection of dainty garments. From them, Ngomo selected a dark maroon, silk chemise with a deep 'v' neck and thin black borders.

Once Fatima had donned it, its appropriateness became immediately apparent. The French girl's bright red lips stood out like wounds, their brightness a marked contrast to the deep toned garment. The blackness of her hair was mirrored by the thin black edging. The garment hung loosely on the girl's curvaceous frame, leaving her breasts free to sway and tremble as she walked, but was tight enough to cling to her well rounded hips. It came down to a few inches below the slave girl's sex. It was pulled tightly across her belly, accenting the beginnings of her thighs.

Ngomo paused only a moment to admire the alluring creature before him. His interest in such things was purely utilitarian. The appearance of the slave would reflect on him.

He spun the girl around and quickly tied her wrists back behind her with a leather thong.

It was the practice to transport the slaves within the palace with their heads covered with a black silk pouch. Ngomo placed one over Fatima's head and drew a string at its opening closed. The slaves had no need to see where they were going and, if they ever were able to slip past the iron gate that barred entrance and exit from the harem, they would have difficulty in deciding which way to go towards freedom. Ngomo attached a short chain with a leather handle, like a dog's lead, to the collar and pulled the French girl forwards.

There were several circuitous routes to the family

quarters, which was Fatima's destination. The girl padded along as she struggled to keep up with Ngomo's long strides. It was disconcerting to be dragged along blindly. The French girl's mind raced with trepidation as to what new indignities and pain awaited her. She knew that she had been decorated for the purpose of presentation, but to whom? Who ruled in this strange place that she had only had a glimpse of? Would the women she had seen before be there? Were they her new owners?

Suddenly, Ngomo brought the girl to a halt. She heard a door being opened and then felt a tug on the leash that led to the collar around her neck. The hallways were made of cool, hard marble, but the room she now entered was soft on her bare feet. She had a sense that other people were in the room. She could hear noises of their activity.

The girl felt herself pulled further into the room and then halted abruptly. She felt Ngomo's hand on her leg, lifting it up and over some barrier. Her other leg was next. Ngomo pressed on her shoulders and she accepted that as a signal to kneel. As she lowered her body, she realized that she was in a wooden trunk or chest. Obediently, she sank down under the pressure of Ngomo's hands until she was bent over, her head touching her knees. Ngomo's hands left her and she heard a lid being lowered above her and then the unmistakable snap of a lock.

There was no way for Fatima to measure the time that she spent locked inside the wooden trunk. She had expected the trunk to be moved, rolled away. It was moved, but only a short distance, dragged along the floor, and then it stopped.

Nervously, the girl awaited future developments. It was as if she was just a thing, to be packaged and stored as her masters desired. Although her small prison was ample enough for her to raise her head to ease the strain on her curved back, the girl was terrified to move. Who knew what penalty she would suffer if she was not found in the position in which she had been left? A slave took no risks; she would endure the painful strain on her muscles.

She could hear voices now, muffled by the walls of her confinement. Was that a woman's voice? Was that singing?

The Queen was delighted when she saw the little, finely carved, wooden chest displayed in the center of the Palace's expansive family room. She was dressed in her splendid finery; the room was bedecked with flowers. There was a large table covered with candies and cakes. When the Emir entered, a portly, grey bearded man, short, but still a powerful presence, all the servants dutifully bowed. The Queen gave a slight nod to her head. The Princess followed him, adorned in her finest new dress, the tops of her beasts modestly displayed. She kissed the Queen and expressed her excitement. Silently, the three awaited the arrival of the guest of honor. After a few moments, the door to the room opened and a young man entered, black haired, trim, a certain dissoluteness in his eyes.

Three voices cried out in unison, "Surprise!"

The young man was Prince Rashan, and it was his twenty-first birthday. He was momentarily startled by the exclamations of his parents and sister, but recovered quickly. He knew that something was up. They would not forget his birthday, the day he became officially a man, the heir to the throne.

His mother smothered him with a huge kiss and an almost crushing hug. Alliyah gave him a peck on the cheek. His father, the Emir, proud of the product of his loins grabbed his shoulders and kissed his mouth. A servant wheeled out a tray of liquid refreshments. The Emir was devoutly religious and so the tray contained, not wine or spirits, but tea and lemonade. The Prince selected lemonade.

After the de rigueur singing of 'Happy Birthday', the Emir was the first to present his gift. He handed his son, a small, decorated box, covered with golden paper and a simple white bow. The Prince bowed to his father. The Queen and the Princess looked on expectantly. Rashan tore off the paper and quickly opened the small cedar box. It was a ring, a fine golden ring with a ruby encrusted signet. It was the seal of the heir to the throne, the symbol of Rashan's manhood and his inheritance. The young man knelt on one knee before his father and kissed his ring. "Father," he said, "I thank you with all of my heart."

A tear in his eye, the Emir leaned over and kissed his son on the head. "Now you are a man, my son. Wear this ring and do me honor."

"Always, Father," the Prince replied.

The tear in the Emir's eye now turned to a gleam. He pulled another box from his robe. It too was wrapped simply, silver paper this time.

"For now," the Emir said, "this may be of more use to you."

129

Rashan quickly unwrapped the present. Inside the small box were the keys to a new Mercedes Sport Convertible. The Emir pointed to the window, and the Prince ran to it and looked down into the courtyard. There was a bright red Mercedes wrapped in broad swaths of yellow ribbon. The Prince thanked his father profusely.

The Princess had a gift too. She handed him a small package, tied neatly with a golden bow. He kissed her on her cheek and opened it quickly. It was a set of sparkling onyx cufflinks, each with a large, shiny ruby in its center. The Prince was a fashion plate and remarked on the Princess's good taste.

And then the Queen grabbed him by his arm. "Oh, Rashan," she said, "I have bought you something very special. Come, come and look at it."

The Prince stepped over to the ornate chest. A large white ribbon had been wrapped around and over it. He stripped away the ribbon and easily released the latch. All four of them were crowded around the box. The Queen placed her hand on Rashan's shoulder, "My son, today you a truly a man. In this chest is truly a man's gift. Use it well."

The Prince nodded to his mother impatiently and then flipped open the lid. There, still kneeling with her forehead to her knees, her brightly decorated hands affixed behind her back, was Fatima. She was startled by the opening of the chest and was startled more by the upraised voices that she heard. The Prince exclaimed loudly, "Oh, mother, what a wonderful gift. Quickly, quickly, let's get her out. I want to see her." He looked up at the Emir. "Is she truly mine?"

The Emir nodded in a fatherly way. "Your mother talked me into it. Enjoy her with my blessing."

Fatima felt her body being pulled up out of the chest. She was brought to her feet and swayed as her stiff legs were extended. Two sets of strong hands, the hands of servants acting at the Prince's behest, lifted her from the box and placed her before her new owner. "Remove the hood!" the Prince exclaimed excitedly.

When the hood was pulled from her head, the frightened slave girl's eyes met the greedy, lustful eyes of her new owner. Her look was no more than a glance, as slave girls had no right to stare their masters in the face. She had seen his excited, gleeful face, the face of a boy, telegraphing the emotions within. But had she seen just a trace of cruelty in those eyes? She sensed that she now belonged to this mere boy, body and soul. He could do with her as he wished, abuse her cruelly to his heart's content. She prayed that there was kindness in him.

The Prince ran his hands down the sides of his new property, hesitating as he felt the gentle curve of her hips. He studied her face intently.

"She's gorgeous, Mother. I am so pleased!"

As the Prince reached to stroke Fatima's trembling breasts, the Emir cleared his throat loudly. "There, there, Rashan, you must respect your mother and sister. There will be plenty of time to inspect your new toy later." The Emir clapped his hands as a signal to the servants. The private birthday ceremony over, the public one was about to begin.

Just before the other guests were admitted, Fatima was discreetly whisked away. Her hood was restored and she was led through another series of corridors. Finally, she was admitted through a doorway and her travels were at an end. One of the Emir's guards, a member of the elite corps of bodyguards sworn to his personal protection, one was never more than an arm's length away, had led Fatima to the Prince's bed chamber. Although Fatima could not see it, it was ornately decorated with long cascading drapery around two floor length windows, a brilliant blue and gold rug, heavy, solid oak furniture stained dark, but with bright golden handles. The bed was a four-posted frame, an oversized mattress and a canopy of white silk that fluttered as the gentle breeze of the air-conditioning swept through the room.

Her chain was affixed to a ring in the corner of the bed, about three feet high. The guard pushed her to her knees, but before doing so, availed himself of a sampling of the Prince's new beauty. He pulled up the maroon chemise and inspected the delicate lips between Fatima's thighs, the soft, firm globes that were her breasts. He did no more than caress them, feeling their fullness. One day he would have a woman like this he thought.

Fatima was left kneeling on the floor, her hands tied behind her back, her sight still restricted by the black hood. She guessed that she was in the boy's bedroom and that she was affixed to his bed. She had no thought as to the guard's unlicensed appreciation of her body. She was only a slave, she knew that, and slaves had no rights. Anyone could do anything to her that they wanted. But what would the boy do? Would he whip her? The French girl resolved to show this boy all of her formidable sexual skills. She would show that she was a treasure, a thing of pleasure. She would give no reason for complaint, no reason for cruelty.

About two hours later, Fatima heard the door to the room opening. She knelt with her back strait, her head held high. Her thighs were spread widely and the lower edge of the chemise rose just above her sex. She jutted out her breasts that they may entice her new owner to his pleasure.

The Prince was a little drunk. True, the Emir had no truck with alcohol, but one of his friends had smuggled a flask of scotch into the party and he had imbibed readily. All of the time he was greeting his father's guests, thanking them for their gifts, charming their wives and daughters, he was thinking of his new slave. He yearned to feel her breasts, her thighs. He wanted to use her, explore the flesh that now was his.

After shutting the door, the Prince took his time in approaching the female on her knees at his bedside. He watched her chest rise and fall, causing her breasts to tremor slightly. He circled the girl, admiring her firm, white thighs, the tightness of her belly. He had his own stock of Scotch secreted in his room and he brought out the bottle and a glass. He gulped back a shot and poured another, all the time his eyes glued on his mother's present. He had used his father's slaves since he was sixteen. They were all beautiful, sexually experienced women. But this one was his. His father disapproved of his excessive use of the female slaves and often rationed him. And he also felt a little disdain from them, despite their lowly status. He would invent reasons to have them beaten, just to spite them. They would return, chastised, but still sullen, resentful at his use of them.

But now, this girl was his. He wanted to see her face again, and he approached the girl and removed her hood. Fatima blinked at the brightness of the room. The Prince grabbed her face and stared at her intently. He entered her mouth with his fingers and withdrew the ball that had kept Fatima silent through most of the day. He pulled her to her feet and then pressed his lips to hers.

Fatima exhilarated at the caress of her master's lips. She welcomed his tongue in her mouth and opened her lips to the Prince's explorations. She felt his manhood stiffen against her as he pressed his body into hers.

Suddenly, the Prince stepped back and, reaching out with both hands, tore the chemise down the middle, exposing Fatima's breasts and belly. He was moved by their beauty. He cupped the breasts in his hands and squeezed them gently. "These are mine," he thought.

Leaning against the bed, the Prince withdrew his manhood from his immaculately pressed white cotton pants. Fatima knew what to do and lowered herself to her knees. Since her hands were still confined behind her back, the French girl had only her mouth to please her master. She edged towards him and leaned forwards, taking the head of his now hard cock in her mouth. She wanted desperately to impress her master with her skills, wanted to entrance him. She nibbled gently at the cock's end and swirled her tongue over its tip. She could sense the Prince stiffen and she heard a soft sigh of pleasure emanate from his lips. She pursed her lips forming a seal around the hardened shaft and slowly pressed forwards, sucking the cock gently deeper into her mouth.

The girl was experiencing a passion of her own. She knew what pleasures this steel hard tool could bring her. Her knees were spread for balance, and she could feel her pussy warming as it engorged with blood, could sense her lower lips separating, her gash lubricating. The Prince's cock was at the back of her mouth now, her lips down to its base. She pushed it into her throat.

Moaning loudly, the Prince locked his hands on his new slave's head. He entwined his fingers in her long, ink black hair and pressed her face into his loins. His cock was throbbing with excitement. He was half sitting on the bed now, his knees too weak to hold his weight. He pulled the girl's head away from him, yearning for the feel of her pliant lips on his rod. As her head was moved backwards, the slave girl dragged the tip of her tongue along the cock's length, ending with a swirl around the cock's head. The Prince began to pull her head back and forth as he thrust his hips into her. He was moaning continuously now as he felt his moment of crisis approach. Faster and faster he moved the head between his thighs. Fatima accommodated her use by tightening her lip's grip around his manhood and opening her throat as the cock jammed up against it.

The Prince called out, "Oh! Oh! Oh!" as a prelude to his tool's eruption. The cock pulsed in Fatima's mouth, a copious discharge of the Prince's fluids flooding it. She pressed her head as far forwards as she could, sheathing the cock in her throat, receiving its discharge directly into her esophagus.

CHAPTER TWELVE

LUNCH

Rukimo and I had lunch on a little veranda overlooking the bay. It was a part of his private quarters and I was, I supposed, honored to be his guest. His quarters sat away from the main resort area and we had to pass through two security checkpoints to get there.

The décor was, as one might expect, sumptuous. The living area was surrounded by a huge wall of glass. The building stood on a promontory and you could see two sides of the island in its view. Two jet-black serving girls greeted us as we entered. They were young, with smooth features, small breasts and long legs. Their sexes were clean shaven and their curly black hair was cropped close to their heads. They both had full, succulent lips. They were kneeling by the door when we entered, eyes downcast, hands upturned on their thighs.

Rukimo nonchalantly rubbed the head of the nearest girl as we passed them by. They stood and followed.

"Harry," Rukimo said as we strolled through the massive room, "what did you think about our little Lois?"

"I don't know," I answered. "It seems unlikely that she was lying."

"Yes," Rukimo countered, "but there was something about her. Of course, we haven't interrogated the other one yet. I've got to find out where they got their information about Morianos' station. If there's a leak in his organization, we need to fix it."

I realized that I was in uncharted territory here. Why was Rukimo confiding in me? Did he suspect something? Did the arrival of the two Americans at Morianos' village in the jungle have anything to do with me? I wondered if one or both of them was meant to be my contact. If so, I was in a world of shit. One of them would talk sooner or later.

Rukimo was studying my face as we strolled out to the veranda. It was a wide expanse of coral pink tile, smooth and glossy. There was a large canopy over it to keep out the midday sun. Rukimo was expecting a response. I decided to play stupid.

"Mr. Rukimo," I said, "I'm afraid that I'm not used to traveling in your league. When I worked for Mr. Blanco, if we had doubts about a guy, we whacked him. There was no sense taking chances. But our little gang was nothing like what you guys have got. I mean, I can hardly take it in. How big is this guy Klitzman?"

Rukimo laughed as he pulled out my chair. "Oh, Harry, let's just say that he's big. This island is just one of his many facilities. I won't give you a list, but anywhere you lived on the globe, you wouldn't have far to go to find one."

I sat and pulled a napkin onto my lap. Rukimo sat opposite me and motioned for the two girls to approach. "Enough business, Harry. How do you like the twins here?"

I looked over the shiny, black skin of the two girls. Their hips were slim, but yet there was a definite curve to their torsos. Their faces were finely sculpted, their eyes were clear. I could smell a faint hint of musk as they stood near me. They were mirror copies of each other, yet the one closer to me seemed a little taller, her breasts just a little larger. Her nipples were a deep red and they jutted out a good inch from her areolas. There was something exotically beautiful about the girls. Each wore the standard steel collar and leather bracelets, but they also had long, bright gold, circular earrings. Their navels sported rings of tiny diamonds.

"They're an eyeful," I said. "Beautiful."

"Oh, yes, I'm awfully proud of them," Rukimo said. "Well trained too. There's actually a story behind them."

A tall, lithesome woman, white, with long blonde hair, emerged from the building. She glided gracefully to our table and made a slight bow to Rukimo. "How may I serve you, master," she said. Her voice was smooth, sulky. She was wearing a bright, multicolored calico skirt low on her hips. Her hair was joined behind her head in a long braid that ended in a knot. Her lips were bright red, her eyes shaded with a delicate blue. She wore nothing on top and her porcelain breasts, large and well rounded, swayed gently as she spoke. It was the first woman I had seen with any clothing. I was surprised.

"This is Tania," Rukimo explained. "She's my major domo. She runs the female staff here." He turned to Tania. "Bring us some lunch, a nice dry Chablis and some fish. We'll have some nuts and cheese while we wait."

Tania bowed again and gracefully exited.

"As I was saying," Rukimo continued, "there's a story behind these two lovelies. Last year we were asked to lend, shall I say, assistance, to a friend of ours, a general in a local army. It seems the President of the republic was seeking to bring what he called 'corruption in the armed forces' under control. Of course, he found that he bit off a little more than he could chew. Our friend, with our help, managed to neutralize the Presidential Guard and install himself as 'the savior of the nation'. The President was shot. His wife now serves as our friend's whore. These are his daughters. The one on the right is Dafina. She was attending Oxford University at the time of the coup. An emergency telegram brought her home. On the left is Deka. She had a job at the American Embassy. Getting her was a little tricky after she claimed political asylum. But we have our ways."

I sensed an uncomfortable shift in the stance of the two young black girls. The one closest to me, Deka, lifted her head slightly and glanced at me quickly. I could see a tremor in her face.

Rukimo spat out a command to the girls in their native language and they ran inside the house. In a moment they were back carrying a thick, red rug. They laid it on the tile next to us, paused for a moment, and then fell into each other's arms.

Their lips locked together and I could see their mouths opening as their tongues intertwined. Their hands descended each other's backs, pausing to stroke the rippling black flesh of their buttocks. Slowly, they descended to their knees and then lay outstretched on the rug. While we awaited our appetizers, we watched the girls conduct a passionate Sapphic display. The taller one was now on top and she spread the legs of her sister. Her fingers danced along the cleft between her thighs as she placed her lips on her breast. The smaller one sighed and raised her chest to meet the oral caress.

I could see the pink interior of the smaller one's pussy as the other spread the soft lips with her fingers. I noticed, as I had not before, that their nether lips were lined with bright gold studs. The studs glinted in the strong mid-day sun. Tania emerged from the house with a small tray of nuts and cheeses along with a shiny, wet bottle of golden wine. Rukimo unceremoniously opened the bottle and poured me a glass. I hesitated to take my eyes off of the passionate display before me. The girls' skins shimmered with a fine sheen of perspiration. They had changed position and were now kissing each other's bellies prefatory to a descent down below. I watched, mesmerized, as their pink tongues lapped the fine, soft hairless skin of their loins and then entered the glistening, wet canals between their legs.

I semiconsciously grabbed a handful of nuts as I admired the luscious display. My temperature was rising and I felt my cock hardening. How was I going to eat with this going on?

I took a long drink of the cold, dry Chablis. Its tart flavor was satisfying and stoked the warmth that was growing in my loins. I heard Rukimo laugh.

"They play well together, eh, Harry?"

"I'll say," I said, not taking my eyes off of the wriggling, sighing pair of impassioned women. The smaller one, the one on the bottom, was the first to begin to moan and squirm. She was joined soon

140

thereafter by her sister. I could see the cheeks of her ass clench, as pulses of pleasure seemed to jolt through her. Were they faking? If they were, it was a very good show.

Finally, the girls' moans became louder and more staccato. Their legs were twitching and their hands clenched each other's backs. Their moans crescendoed and then began to fade. I gulped back the remainder of my wine.

As the girls slumped apart, I noticed Tania waiting patiently, holding a covered tray. Rukimo's white teeth were flashing as he grinned in appreciation of the show. He looked at me conspiratorially and then nodded to Tania.

The tall, white girl approached the table and, holding the tray with one hand, lifted the lid. On it was a steaming, pink colored fish, filleted, sitting on a bed of saffron rice. Small roasted tomatoes circled the rice bed. It looked and smelled delicious.

Tania bent over as she allowed me to serve myself from the tray. Her breasts swayed gently as she waited for me to fill my plate. I noticed small sapphire studs in her ears.

Rukimo and I ate silently. The fish had a delicate smoked flavor. It melted in my mouth. When we had finished, Tania appeared, as if by magic, and cleared away our plates. The bottle of wine was three quarters empty and my head had begun to swim in the heat, exacerbated by the residual hard on I was sporting. Rukimo grinned at me.

"There's only one way to finish off a fine meal like this, Harry," he said. He looked at the twins who had remained entwined, caressing each other almost lovingly. They needed no further instruction, leaping to their feet and scrambling towards us. The short one knelt at my feet and dipped her head under the table. Her hands parted my robe and her mouth engulfed my steel hard cock.

I almost swooned as the hot mouth and soft tongue descended the length of my tool. I spread my legs wide and placed my hands on the black haired head between my thighs. I looked over to see Rukimo similarly occupied. As the girl's lips pressed hard against the bulbous head of my cock, I let my head roll back and closed my eyes. I felt soft hands caressing my thighs as the girl's tongue swirled around the tip of my manhood. Maybe tomorrow, or the day after, I would be able to calmly revel in the oral ministrations of a beautiful slave girl, but not today. I had more than three years worth of lust to satisfy. I felt my juices rising and I began to moan. As my penis jerked and pulsed, spilling my seed into the energetic mouth, wave after wave of pleasure washed over me. I ended with a long, satisfied sigh.

Rukimo was still busily milking his cock with the taller black girl's mouth. I could hear little cries emerge from her as he, holding her black carpeted head between his hands, jammed his cock against the back of her throat. Tania had returned and was watching silently, her face a mask of indifference. The girl between my legs was sucking gently on my flaccid penis, stroking my balls gently. I could feel the blood stirring again.

It was somewhat disconcerting to have my dick in this girl's mouth while the blond woman stood sphinxlike next to me. I admired her soft, inviting breasts and the way her belly curbed inwards near her hips. The scandalously short skirt hid away her sex and upper thighs and I could not help but wonder what lay beneath. It was funny that I had been inundated by visions of beautiful, naked flesh all day long, and yet here I was, tantalized by what I could not see and probably could not have. I had to guess that she was Rukimo's personal property. And I didn't want to fuck with Rukimo.

I was drawn from my lustful appraisal of Tania by Rukimo's loud grunts. He was coming at last. I saw him press the black head down onto his loins, pushing his quite ample manhood deep into the young girl's throat. He held it there as he rolled his head back, luxuriating in his passionate discharge. The girl's body tensed due to the cessation of the flow of air to her lungs. I could see her hands clench, the muscles of her back contract and stiffen. I had to give her credit, though. She moved her head not an inch.

Finally, Rukimo released the head he had held so firmly to its task. My cock was hardening, but I sensed that my luncheon was just about over. Rukimo snapped his fingers and the two black sisters scurried back to their rug.

"Ahhhhh, Harry," Rukimo sighed. There's nothing like a well-trained mouth. How was yours?"

"Perfect," I replied.

"And now I think I'll have my siesta, Harry. Enjoy the rest of the afternoon, take a walk around," Rukimo said. "Get laid."

I laughed. "Sure Mr. Rukimo," I said. "I'll do that."

As I got up from my chair Rukimo spoke to Tania.

"Go to my bedroom and wait for me there," he told her. "And bring the number two whip."

Tania stiffened and I detected a momentary trace of fear in her face. It was gone after a split second. "Yes, master," was all she said.

CHAPTER THIRTEEN

THE PRINCE REVEALED

The Prince was suitably impressed with the oral skills of his new slave. Her rubbed her head with his hand, petting her, as she coaxed the last few drops of cum from his slowly detumescing organ. When he had regained his senses, the Prince pushed the slave girl's head back and drew her to her feet. He pulled the covers down to the foot of the bed and then pushed her onto it. The remnants of her chemise were gathered around her bound wrists. She lay there in anxious anticipation of her further use while the Prince stripped off his clothes. He joined the woman on the bed and spread his tall, taut frame alongside her. She could feel the heat of his body pressing against her. He grabbed her by the hair and kissed her lips, running his tongue inside her mouth. Her eyes closed, the young woman eagerly accepted his passionate embrace.

The Prince ran his left hand down Fatima's body, caressing her breasts, stroking her belly. He covered her sex with his hand and probed within. Fatima's cunt was plush and hot. She moaned as his hand enflamed her. Her nipples were taut with passion, she yearned for her master's cock.

Running his lips down along Fatima's neck, sucking gently on her skin, he descended to her breasts. While his left hand manipulated her flush sex, his other hand circled her right breast, squeezing it, first gently and then harder. He bit down on the nipple softly, sending an electric charge throughout the young girl's body.

His lips went lower and lower, scraping along her stomach and down to the apex of her moist canal. Shifting his body so that he was between her legs, he spread them widely so that he could examine the engorged lips, the tender, pink center. The Prince inhaled the sweet odor of the perfume that had been applied there. His cock had risen again and ached for insertion in a warm, moist place. As he ran his tongue inside the labial lips and up and down the expanding crevasse between them the girl was virtually apoplectic with pleasure. She had prayed that her new master would appreciate her charms, would revel in her softness, would enjoy her compliant sexuality. But she hadn't dreamt that he would give her pleasure like this.

The Prince ran his hands along the inside of the girl's widespread thighs as he continued to agitate her pussy with his tongue. She began to rock her hips in anticipation of her incipient orgasm. Quickly, the Prince withdrew his tongue and, pulling her right leg over her left, turned the girl to her belly. He pulled back her hips until her lower portals were exposed to his use. Kneeling on the bed, her forehead pressed into the mattress, Fatima waited to be filled. She felt the Prince's cock press against the dainty star of her ass, and loosened her muscles in aide of his ease of penetration. She was a well-trained slut. Many weeks of whippings and callous rapes had brought her to the point where her rear entrance could be used almost as easily as her front. The Prince enjoyed the benefit of her skills, as he was able to thrust his cock past the tight ring of flesh easily.

Fatima moaned as the Prince's steel hard cock filled her. There was no question but that she had come to enjoy a good ass fucking. The friction of the pistoning of a hot cock against the sensitive tissues of her anus sent wave after wave of pleasurable impulses to her crevasse, and in turn, to her body. The Prince, too, enjoyed the fine art of sodomy. He thrilled to the feeling of soft warmth that surrounded his rampant pole and the tight pressure brought to bear by the narrow portal. He pumped into Fatima's bowels, first slowly, and then with increasing intensity. He took joy at the vision of the tightly bound wrists as the girl's hands writhed in evidence of her passion. The girl began to utter small, shrill cries as he rammed his cock home repeatedly. The cries increased in intensity as he felt her bucking against him.

When he sensed that she was coming, he intensified his efforts, his mind clouding with pleasure. Suddenly he could hold back no more and he shot a hot load of sperm deep inside the excited woman.

Fatima felt the warmth spread within her and her orgasm recommenced. What joy she felt that she had brought her master to pleasure and that he had stirred such a passionate release in her! It was as a wish come true! He would treasure her, yearn for her, and she would please him like a lustful whore.

When the Prince ceased his movements, the couple lay silently in place, their chests heaving, blood still pounding in their brains. The Prince bent forward, leaning his chest against the girl's sweaty back. When he felt his penis slip from the girl's rear, he disengaged himself and lay back on the bed. He caressed the cheeks of her ass with one hand as he luxuriated in the calm after the storm. The girl lay still, enjoying the afterglow of her orgasms. She would not move again until instructed, but she would do whatever her master commanded.

Fatima would not have been so content if she could have read her master's mind. Yes, he had enjoyed his sexual bout with his new property, but he had just begun to take his pleasure with her. As he rose from his supine position, his innate cruelty began to emerge.

The Prince rose from the bed and refreshed his glass of scotch. He downed it quickly, enjoying the fiery bite as it went down his throat. He glanced up at the chain that he had had installed in the ceiling in the middle of the room. The chain ran through an eyebolt and then across the ceiling to another eyebolt and then down the wall. At the bottom of the wall lay sufficient length of chain so that it could be lowered in the middle of the room. He had had some of his father's slaves dance to the whip there, but his father was particular how his slaves were marked up, and he could rarely go beyond a mere warming of their flesh. But tonight, all restraint was washed away. He would be the judge of what marks were to be worn by his slave and how they got there. He wanted to hear her scream in agony.

Fatima heard the jangle of the chain as it was lowered from the ceiling. She dared not look to discover its source. But it was a familiar sound and it did not bode her well. As she sensed the Prince approaching the bed, her throat began to constrict with fear. Was her idyll about to dissolve into terror? There was a deep, sinking feeling in her stomach.

The Prince leaned over the bed and untied Fatima's wrists, discarding the torn and ragged maroon chemise. He then pulled her from the bed and dragged her to where the foreboding chain descended from the ceiling. The French girl cringed when she saw it and the open bracelets that dangled from its end. She started to pull away from the Prince's vice like grip on her arm. It was an involuntary motion, prompted by panic and dread. The Prince lashed out, striking her across the face with his hand. The unanticipated blow knocked the girl senseless.

"Come here, whore," the Prince growled. "Come and take the beating you deserve."

The French girl did not understand the words, but understood their meaning. She dreaded the whip. She would do anything to avoid it. She had seen almost countless women piteously beg and plead to be spared the painful kiss of the lash. None of them had been. She resolved not to beg and whine. She would submit. It was the only means left to her, a lowly slave, to assert her humanity, to preserve what little pride she had left, to stoically accept whatever her master could dole out.

She could not prevent the tears forming in her eyes or the involuntary grimace that crossed her face. The Prince locked her hands into the bracelets and pulled the chain until her hands were held far above her head, her feet barely touching the ground. He affixed a strap around her ankles to hold her legs together and bound it to a ring in the floor, immobilizing her. He wanted her as still as possible so that his blows landed where he aimed them.

Once the girl was postured in the desired manner, the Prince made a circle around her body. She was a beautiful beast, he thought. His cock had risen and he stroked it as he contemplated the girl's misery. He could smell her fear, could see it in the sweat that was dripping down her body. He went over to the long, low credenza against the wall and poured himself another tall scotch. He took a long pull on it, putting a sharper edge on his lust. He opened the credenza and removed a long, thin rattan cane, a short, many thonged whip and a thick, heavy riding crop. "Which one shall I use first?" he thought. He chose the whip. It would warm her up for the cane, which would mark her with long, red lacerations. And then the riding crop to cause deep purple bruises in her skin.

The Prince finished off his glass of scotch and, placing the cane and the riding crop down on the credenza, stepped over to the girl. She had been watching him with desperate intensity, mesmerized by his every motion. The Prince rubbed his hand over her breasts, squeezing them harshly. He took a nipple in his mouth and sucked on it long and hard. The girl could feel the heat of his naked body next to hers. The anticipation of her torment proved too much and she began to emit a low, piteous whine. The Prince looked up in her face and laughed.

"Are you ready to begin?" he taunted her. "I'm ready."

The Prince stepped away and swung the thonged whip, landing its stiff, knotted ends across the girl's back. The girl stiffened and moaned. Her lips were trembling with pain and fear as she struggled to accept mutely whatever the Prince dealt out to her. Another blow of the whip crossed her bound legs, braising her thighs. Another blow across her back and another on the thighs. The Prince struck blow after blow in rapid succession. He moved so that he could whip her defenseless breasts, her belly and the front of her thighs. Fatima was mewing and crying as she suffered the burning pain. Her body was twisting vainly to assuage the impact of the blows.

As he continued his vicious assault, the Prince's eyes glazed over with lust. The girl's body was turning a bright pink where the repeated blows had fallen. It was more exciting than he had imagined. Each tiny cry, each involuntary flinch, each teardrop that he wrested from the girl fueled his cruel passion.

The Prince paused to catch his breath. Fatima swung listlessly in her chains, sobbing lightly. She looked up at the distorted visage of her assailant and knew that she could expect no mercy. He had just begun to torment her.

When the first stroke of the cane landed, it let out a loud 'crack' that echoed in the room. The fiery pain shot through the girl. A loud groan escaped her lips. A bright red line had formed across her tenderized breasts. Her tear-filled eyes pleaded with her assailant. She bit her lips to prevent an outpouring of fruitless entreaties. Another lash struck her, this time across her thighs. Her groan became more of a shriek. After the third blow from the thin rod, she lost all will to control herself, all pride left her. Fatima screamed loudly and began to cry out and beg piteously. "Please, please," she begged in English. "Please!" When the fourth kiss of the lash like cane kissed her rear, the girl lost her English, what little she had, and began to beg piteously in French.

Pausing to enjoy the girl's entreaties, the Prince admired his handiwork. Long red lines of lacerated wounds had formed about the girl's body. He had gone far past anything he had done before. He wanted to go farther. The Prince increased the speed and intensity of the blows. Fatima lost any ability to speak as a steady stream of pain burned through her. She was screaming now, uncontrollably. Tears streamed down her face. "Ahhhhhhhhhhh!" she cried

Finally, the rain of blows stopped. The Prince was sweating profusely. The effort of whipping his slave left him panting and trembling with lust. The girl hung, lifeless but for the loud, soulful sobbing and the heaving of her chest. She was covered with long, red welts, some of them oozing blood. The Prince gave her a few seconds to gather her wits. The crop was next and he wanted her to enjoy every blow.

Another shot of Scotch was in order. The Prince dropped the cane and poured out three fingers of the clear, amber liquid. It went down in one gulp. His head was beginning to cloud, but he shook it off. He took the riding crop in his hand.

Fatima raised her head and saw the next implement of her torment. She knew that the riding crop caused deep, painful bruises that lasted many days. Reaching deep down inside herself, the girl summoned the last vestiges of her strength. She would suffer the blows in silence, she resolved. She would give the cruel man no more of herself.

Rashan struck the girl across the back with all of the strength he could summon. It was good that he was tired and drunk, for the desire to inflict pain was stronger than his arm. In spite of this, the riding crop caused a loud 'thump' when it landed. Fatima received the painful blow stoically. A second, third and fourth blow struck her. The pain coursed through her, but other than a small cry as each blow landed, she remained silent. Ten times the Prince landed the thick, hard instrument on her body. Each stroke sent a sickening wave of pain through the girl. In spite of herself, Fatima let out a long, doleful moan as the final blow landed.

Seeing that he could evoke no further screams of pain from his slave, Rashan cast the riding crop aside. Despite all of his liquor, his cock was still rampant. He would fuck his whore once more.

He released the sagging girl's wrists from the cuffs and she fell instantly to the floor. He freed her feet from the ring in the floor, grabbed her hair and dragged her to the bed. "Get up you cunt!" he yelled as he pulled on her arms. Fatima's instinct for self-preservation gave her the power to push with her rubbery legs as she was raised upwards. The Prince flung her onto the bed and untied her ankles. He pounced on her body as she rolled to her back. He pushed her legs apart with his thighs and pressed his cock into her hole.

The girl was moist, receptive, as many months of training and conditioning had taught her to be. She was even grateful for the flush of incipient pleasure caused by the steel hard rod pressed inside her. Giving herself over to pleasure, the only thing left to her, she rose to meet the Prince's thrusts. He grabbed her hands and held then above her head and pressed his lips onto hers. She opened her mouth willingly, earnestly seeking to raise her passions. It did not take long for the Prince to approach fulfillment of his lust. Fatima too, was close, and she raised her knees, pushing her heels hard in to the bed. She desperately pounded her hips into his. He owed her this, she thought; she earned this. As the Prince stiffened, his cock pulsing and throbbing with pleasure, the French girl came too. She sucked on the Prince's tongue hungrily as her pussy knotted into blissful contraction after contraction.

Finally, it was over. The Prince's passion was spent. Fatima lay dazed and exhausted, all energy drained from her. The man rolled off of her and quickly sunk into a drunken stupor. Mercifully, she fell asleep.

After about an hour, as the Prince's snores resounded throughout, two silent, light footed servants crept into the room. The scotch was put away, the whips stowed back in the credenza. The torn remnants of the chemise the slave girl had worn were recovered. Fatima felt herself shaken awake. She was startled, panicked. But one of the self-effacing men placed his hand over her mouth and whispered "Shhhhhhhhhh!"

The girl was quickly, but gently, rolled onto her stomach. She felt her hands being tied behind her back and her ankles joined. A hand pulled her head back and a leather ball was forced into her mouth. A black silk hood descended over her head and was tied off at the neck. As the girl tearfully rued her helpless fate, the two men gracefully and quietly glided across the room, dimmed the lights and closed the door behind them. Wracked with sobs, she cried herself back to sleep.

CHAPTER FOURTEEN

THE DUTCH GIRL

The midday sun beat down unmercifully on the now empty patios and verandas as I left Rukimo's abode. The morning breeze had disappeared, and everyone had gone inside. The only other persons I could see were the ubiquitous guards and even they had managed to find shade. I decided to take a little siesta myself and wandered over to the supervisor's dormitory. I passed through the lounge area, and, except for a number of slaves chained to rings along the walls, and a foursome of rough looking fellows playing poker, it was deserted.

I walked down the curved hallway, looking for my card in the slot by the door. When I found it, I entered. The blonde haired girl who had been given the ridiculous name of Tulip was kneeling in the middle of the room, her hands resting on her thighs, palms up, her back erect. Her eyes were downcast, her head bowed. She was a beautiful creature, no more than nineteen or twenty. Her heavy, plump breasts had large red areolae, with flat, dime sized nipples. Her skin was as white as cream and seemed as smooth and rich. I sensed her nervousness at my presence, an expectancy of demands intolerant of lassitude.

Stepping up to the girl, I placed my hand under her chin and raised her face. "Look at me," I said. Her eyes were pale blue with flecks of white in them, giving them an almost star like quality. A very light tint of blue covered her eyelids, complementing her eyes, which were outlined with a thin line of black. Her eyelashes were long and curled and a faint tint of blush was on her cheeks. Her parted lips were painted a dull red, echoing the hue of her nipples and areolae.

"I want to take a bath," I told her.

"Yes, master," she replied. She rose gracefully and stepped quickly into the bathroom. As she walked away from me, I admired her long, narrow back and the tight, solid globes of her ass. I removed my robe and heard the water begin to splash into the tub. I strode into the bathroom and was startled by the luxurious décor. The tub was large, sunken into the floor. A shower was set in one end with a gold plated faucet and handles below it. The room was lined with a wainscoting of copper colored tiles, the upper walls papered with red, yellow and blue swirls.

The tub filled rapidly and I could see the steam rising from the heated water. The girl stood in the tub expectantly. I descended the three steps into the tub and sat down in the water, my back laying against a sloped side. The heated water drained all of my energy as my muscles went limp. I sighed with pleasure. This was the life.

I dozed off almost immediately; I don't know how long, but for at least ten or fifteen minutes. I awoke at the sound of water being added to the tub by the girl, to maintain the luxuriant temperature. Groggily, I drew myself to my feet and stepped towards the faucets where a bar of creamy white soap lay in a golden dish. I heard the timid, tentative voice of my servant, "Master, may I wash you?"

I nodded affirmatively, and the girl lifted a large soft sponge from the water and approached me. I closed my eyes as I felt the sponge dragged across my broad back. The girl's body was pressed up close to mine as she meticulously soaped my shoulders and arms. She then did the back of my thighs and my ass. The blonde girl dutifully crossed in front of me and soaped my front. When she reached my cock and balls, she rubbed the soap in her hands and delicately massaged me there. She was kneeling in the water, her breasts rubbing up against my thighs. Her entire being seemed devoted to her task.

She left my manly appendage just as it had begun to harden. She rubbed the sponge along the inside of my thighs. The water was up to just below my knees and when the girl's efforts reached there, she gracefully lifted my legs so that she could wash my feet. She massaged my feet with her surprisingly strong hands. I was awash with a mesmerizing pleasure as she manipulated the toes and dug her fingers deep into the bottom of my feet. I had to place my hands on her head to keep my balance as my mind swum with the delectable sensations.

When she had finished my feet, the girl urged me over to the shower and, turning the spigot on, rinsed my body. Apparently loathe to disturb my reverie, she whispered "Will the master lower himself so I can wash his hair?"

I complied wordlessly with her request. I knelt in the water, my haunches resting on my thighs. The girl spread a ginger scented dollop of soap in my hair and massaged it thoroughly into my scalp. Her strong fingers drove all thought from my brain, all sensation from my body, except for their enervating, almost hypnotic rhythm. When she was done with the shampoo and had washed it from my head, she applied a similarly scented cream rinse. She worked it into my scalp and resumed her massage of my head.

When she had finished, she requested that I stand and commenced to rub a lightly scented body lotion into my skin. She started, as before, on my back, running her strong hands cross my shoulder muscles, down my spine and across my rear. When she had finished the back of my legs, she came to my front, covering my arms and my almost hairless chest. As she massaged the lotion into my body, she pressed hers tantalizingly close to me. The steam from the bathwater befogged the room, creating a dream-like atmosphere. When she began to cover my thighs, first the fronts and then the insides, I felt her lips brush against the head of my cock. Obediently, it sprang to life. I looked down just as the beautiful blonde girl, a sheen of water covering her most desirable flesh, leaned forwards and gobbled the head of my now hardened dick into her mouth.

The wave of pleasure that shot through me was so intense that I had to close my eyes and arch my back. I steadied myself by again latching onto the head that now slowly and artfully bobbed on my cock. Her hand cupped my scrotum and massaged the small twin orbs within. Her tongue danced on my tool, sliding down its length and then up again on the other side. The expert mouth then engulfed my pulsing rod, consuming it to its length. I felt the tight, hot constriction of her throat. The girl moaned, sending pleasurable vibrations down the length of my rock solid instrument. I felt my fluids rising and I groaned with pleasure. A precum tingle passed through me, starting from the warm sac that the girl was delicately massaging, and expanding through my body to my brain. As I came, I could feel the passage of my semen as it was pumped through my penis and into the welcoming mouth. The girl sucked long and hard as jolt after jolt of almost painful pleasure passed through me. As the last few diminishing pulses throbbed in my cock, the girl circled it with her other hand, pumping it softly as she licked the final drops of sperm from its tip.

When I had recovered from my semi-conscious stupor, I looked down at the girl. Her eyes were expectantly peering up at me. I leaned over and pulled her to her feet and kissed her lips. She whispered to me timidly, "Was the master pleased?"

"Oh, yes," I answered. "Very much."

"Let me dry you master and then you can rest," she said with somewhat more confidence. I let her lead me by the hand from the tub and stood docilely as she patted me dry. She then led me from the bathroom and over to the bed. She pulled down the cool, white sheets and gently guided me down until I lay there supine. She quickly dried her own body with a towel and jumped in beside me. She pressed her body against mine, draping her arm across my chest. I was asleep almost instantly.

When I awoke, I was alone in the bed. The strong, midday light had dimmed. For a second I thought I was back in the joint and that all of this had been a dream. But I knew I was awake when I saw the blonde girl kneeling at the foot of the bed in what I came to learn later was presentation position. I remembered her well trained mouth and my cock stirred.

"Come here," I said.

Without further instruction, the buxom girl crawled into bed with me. I drew off the white, silk sheet and had the girl spread herself out by my side. I had come already four times this day, but the little boy raised his head nonetheless. I leaned over and draping my leg over hers, took her stiff, button like nipple in my mouth. Her breasts were like pillows, soft and plump. I ran my calloused hand down her side and the flank of her thigh. She moaned as I pulled hard on her teat with my teeth.

When I was sentenced to a lifetime prison sentence, I had believed that I would never feel the pleasure of the skin of a beautiful woman's against mine as long as I lived. It was heaven. She ran her soft hand across my shoulder and down my back. I switched to the other breast and laid my stomach onto hers. I could feel her breathing beneath me, the beating of her heart. My left hand found the center of her thighs and gently stroked the hairless mound. I drew another moan from the girl as I teased her nipple with my tongue and gently massaged her other breast with my right hand. Her body stirred beneath mine.

I looked up and saw both passion and uncertainty in the girl called Tulip's face. Her mouth was pursed into a pout as I continued to massage her breast, the firm flesh more than filling my hand. But there was worry in her eyes. And I realized that for this girl each sexual encounter was a test, a test of her training, her obedience. Pain and torment were always but a moment away for her. I ran my other hand through her golden hair, spread about her head on the pillow like a corolla. I placed my hand on the side of her face and stroked her cheek gently. I felt pity for this frightened girl. I looked into her eyes and kissed her lips tenderly. "It's all right," I whispered. "It's all right."

Her eyes softened and she smiled gratefully. She reached her hand behind my head and pulled my lips back to hers, opening her mouth and drawing in my tongue. It was my turn to moan as her hot tongue inflamed me. I moved my legs between hers and, grabbing my stiffened cock, rubbed its head along her lower lips. She was moistened and her lips slid open easily. I slowly eased myself inside her. As I felt her soft, hot tunnel envelop me, I sighed with pleasure.

I began to slowly rock my piece backwards and forwards within her. Each traverse of her channel sent ripples of excitement through me. I could feel her hips grinding slowly, matching my almost torpid pace. Gradually, the pace quickened. I could not teeter on the brink of passion for too long. The girl's tongue danced against mine as she circled me with her arms, drawing me tightly in. Her legs curled around mine pulling me deeper into her loins.

I was overwhelmed now with lust. I slammed my hips against hers and grabbed the sides of her face with my hands. She was breathing heavily and pouring little intermittent cries into my mouth. Again and again I drove my cock deep into her womb. It seemed that all of me was centered there, that all the nerve endings of my body were wired to my manhood. Suddenly, the girl's little cries became shouts. Her fingers dug deep into my back, her legs held me vice-like between them. As her hips ground hard against mine I let loose a stream of hot cum deep within her. Our lips had parted and I was calling out my pleasure loudly. Our mutual orgasms seemed to last forever, our bodies merged into one writhing, shuddering beast. When the pulsing of my long, thick rod subsided, I could still feel the hard, rhythmic contractions of her pussy. Finally, we lay still together, intertwined, overwhelmed by our spent passion.

CHAPTER FIFTEEN

ONE WOMAN'S PLEASURE

Fatima's morning began with a resounding slap on her ass. The Prince was awake and while he was awake his whore was not permitted sleep. The girl gave a sharp cry, deadened by the leather ball in her mouth and the silk sack over her head. She felt the Prince get up off of the bed and heard him enter the bathroom and pee. The shower began to run and she heard the sounds of him stepping in. She had suffered terribly the night before, worse than she had suffered since her first day as a slave. The sound of the running water gave her some slight comfort as it meant that the Prince was engaged in another activity and could not harm or abuse her.

When the shower ended, Fatima's stomach began to turn. She knew that it was unlikely that her tormentor would commence his day's activities, if he had any that is, without directing his attention to his new plaything. The Prince emerged from the bathroom drying himself off with a heavy, thick cotton towel. He looked at the red striped woman who lay on his bed. Maybe he had overdone it a little, he thought. But he had derived immeasurable pleasure from it. He resolved that it would not be the only night she would be tortured. In the meantime, the shower had relieved his hangover and he was randy. He wanted to fuck his new slave. That's what she was for, wasn't it?

Not bothering to untie the girl, the prince swung her legs off of the bed and turned her torso so that she was face down, lying horizontally across the mattress. He bracketed her legs with his. Her body was folded on the bed's edge in such a way to present her rear globes and the hidden entrance between them nicely. No need to untie her ankles, it would be tighter this way.

Fatima felt the head of the Prince's cock probing at her rear opening. With her ankles tied, the entrance was constricted and narrow. As the Prince pressed forward, Fatima felt her tender flesh being stretched and torn. Although the way was difficult, the Prince just pressed harder until he was admitted to the her bowels. She squealed in pain as the hard sword of flesh delved inside her. Once inside, the Prince began to saw his stiff cock across the pursed lips of her anus. The mattress rocked the girl's body up and down with each of his thrusts. She struggled at her bonds, rebelling against this new abuse.

The Prince's hands were on the bed on either side of the girl's body and his locked elbows kept him poised above her. He admired her twisting hands as they involuntarily conveyed her dismay. The hole was tight and the ring of flesh clung firmly to his shaft. He groaned as he felt his orgasm build. When he felt the pulsing of his member, he drove it home to the hilt, letting his sperm jet deep inside her.

The French girl welcomed the Prince's release. She gratefully felt him withdraw. The stretched lips burned as the thick member drew across them.

The Prince wiped his now flaccid tool with the

towel he had used to dry himself and tossed it aside. He had things to do today. He dressed quickly, leaving Fatima draped across the bed. She dared not stir without instruction. When he was fully dressed, smart black pants, a loose, blue cotton shirt, fine black, leather Italian shoes, he rang for a servant. To his surprise Ngomo entered the room.

"Yes, Ngomo, what is your business here?" he inquired.

"If you Lordship will permit, I have come to retrieve the slave," the tall coffee colored eunuch answered.

"Never mind that," the Prince said disdainfully. "She is to remain here."

"It is as your Lordship wishes," Ngomo replied deferentially. "But if salve is not placed on her wounds, she will scar. And she needs to be fed and bathed, and to rest, so that she may serve you again tonight."

Rashan felt that he was being out maneuvered by the slave master. He looked back at the girl for a few seconds and then turned to Ngomo. "All right. But have her back here before dinnertime."

"As your Lordship commands," Ngomo said with a slight bow. He despised the Prince, his Western ways, his excesses. This girl was a delicate flower to be enjoyed, not a cow to be beaten for no reason. The eunuch was aware that men took pleasure in administering pain to women. The Emir often had the slaves whipped for his amusement. But everything was to be taken in moderation. He said a silent prayer for the Emir's long life.

Fatima heard the discourse between her tormentor and the slave master. She recognized his deep baritone voice. She knew that she was the subject of their debate and hoped that the resolution of their disagreement would not visit more torment and abuse on her. She felt her ankles being untied and then strong arms lifting her from the bed. She sagged when she was brought to her feet. The Slave Master held her body close to his until she was able to balance herself. A leash was clipped to her collar, she was hooded and then led from the room.

For the next two weeks, Fatima satisfied the Prince's pleasures nightly. Each night she hoped that her considerable sexual skills would dissuade him from further torment of her body. Some nights, the nights that he was not drunk, and they were few, she was able to deflect his violent disposition by the slow, mesmerizing service of his manhood. She had a dexterous cunt and a wonderful mouth. Her rear entrance was supple and she knew how to grip his tool tightly. Each time he orgasmed, she would subtly and slowly reignite his passion, stroking his instrument, rubbing her breasts against him, writhing her torso atop his.

She allowed herself to be carried away with lust as he pounded his cock inside her loins or her ass. She knew that only the most passionate of embraces would entrance this demon who owned her. It made tolerable the callous exploitation of her flesh.

During the days, Fatima was allowed to freely consort with her fellow slaves. She treasured her times with the three slave girls who had comforted her on her first day. They taught her the simple rules of their cruel prison. Foremost of all was the need to obey. There was another French girl there and Fatima was relieved to have someone to talk to. It was forbidden to speak of their former lives in any but the most general of terms.

Most of the other slave girls were sympathetic of Fatima's fate as the property of the cruel and sadistic Prince. Compared to him, the Emir was kind. The only unpleasant aspect of spending her days in the harem was the Spanish girl. She lorded it over the others and on more than one occasion had delivered unwarranted and unexpected blows to Fatima.

One day, however, the Spanish girl received her comeuppance. She had been taken to service the Emir at his afternoon siesta. When she returned, there were bright red stripes about her body, the evidence of a severe lashing. When her hood was removed, it was seen that she was masked by a leather gag. Only her forlorn eyes could be seen.

Ngomo unceremoniously pushed her to the floor and attached a chain from the ceiling to her ankles. He pulled the chain taut and she rose from the floor. Ngomo took from his belt a thick leather encased crop and commenced belaboring her body with it ruthlessly. The Spanish girl groaned and shrieked as the force of the blows caused her body to sway back and forth, her voice stifled by her gag.

When Ngomo was done, he left her hanging there for several hours. Seeing their chance at revenge, the slave girls repeatedly and viciously slapped and punched her defenseless form. Even Fatima joined in, pinching and twisting the upside down girl's breasts and nipples, cursing at her in French.

When Ngomo returned, all of the girls fell dutifully to the floor, pressing their heads down and crossing their arms behind their backs. Ngomo lowered the Spaniard to the floor, rehooded her and dragged her from the room. None of the girls ever learned what the Spanish had done to merit Ngomo's wrath. She was never seen again.

There finally came a time when Prince Rashan did not call for Fatima's services. Even Ngomo had developed sympathy for the girl. He entered the harem one afternoon. The girls all made their supplicating bows. He called out Fatima's name. As required, and as she had done now a good two dozen times, Fatima rose from her kneeling position, ran to Ngomo and fell down at his feet, her hands behind her, head to the floor. She expected the silken bag to be affixed over her head and her hands to be tied prefatory to being led to the Prince's chambers. Each time she had run to Ngomo, her stomach had churned. Her revulsion at the Prince and his cruelty to her was complete. She prayed every day that he would not call her, cried every morning when she was returned.

But this day, Ngomo did not prepare her for transport. Instead he announced matter of factly that her master had gone away on a trip and would not be back for ten days. He then turned and left.

Fatima was shocked that Ngomo would break protocol to give a slave any information regarding her future. But after a moment, her joy overcame her surprise. Ten whole days! She was free of her cruel and heinous master for ten whole days! She rushed back to the harem common room and hugged Gelela for joy. They had become constant lovers and the best of friends. Gelela joined Fatima's celebration.

The next few days were like heaven to Fatima. She rose leisurely each day, refreshed and contented. For the first time she was able to spend the night wrapped in the arms of her lover. With the Spaniard gone, there was no reason for fear from her. Gelela and the others were subject to being called for by the Emir, but there were seven slaves and he could not have all of them every night. Fatima was happy to be able to greet Gelela on her return from the Emir's bed following the two evenings that she spent there during this period.

One night, all of the slaves, save Fatima, were called to serve. The Emir was having a banquet and the girls were to entertain his guests. For the first time, Fatima was all alone in the harem. It was a strange experience not to be surrounded by a bevy of nearly naked women. Fatima prepared herself for a long and lonely night. But about an hour after the other girls had been led in a bound and hooded procession from the harem, Ngomo returned. Fatima was in the dormitory, reclining on her bed when she heard his deep voice call her name.

The French girl sprinted to the common room and fell to her knees before the Slave Master. Her mind was afire with fear. Had the Prince returned? He was not due for another three days. Her whole body tingled with apprehension. Was her ordeal to start anew?

Ngomo hooded and bound the girl and, after leashing her, led her from the harem. As usual, Ngomo's strides were long and quick and she had to scurry blindly behind him. She was brought to a halt while a door was opened and led inside. She had steeled herself to her fate, but something told her that she was not in the Prince's bedroom. Another hand grabbed her leash and tugged on it gently. The pace was then more leisurely. Fatima smelt the scent of perfume. It was a woman leading her.

She passed through several more corridors and through a series of doors. She was brought to a halt and her hood was removed. She was in a large bedroom, decorated in a feminine style. There were long pink gauze curtains on the windows, a soft red carpet and large paintings of flowers and scenes of nature on the walls. The walls themselves were rose colored. In the middle of one of the walls was a large canopied bed with a blue and white flowered bedspread and large fluffy pillows.

It was the Queen who held her leash. She looked the slave girl over, making sure that he makeup was complete. Fatima was dressed in a sheer, coffee colored teddy. Her nails had been painted a dark brown and a dark red lipstick had been applied to her lips, nipples and labia. Her shiny black hair had been trimmed to frame her face. An ironclad harem rule was that all slaves must be ready to serve at all times. Fatima, even though she had not expected to be called out tonight had dutifully complied with the rule and she was a delectable vision. The Queen smiled at her and caressed her breast saying something soft and sweet sounding in Arabic.

Fatima was led over to the bed and her leash removed. She knelt in submission. After a few moments the door to the bathroom opened and the Princess Alliyah emerged, dressed in a flowing, sheer, green and white nightgown. Her black hair was tied in a long braid behind her head. She looked nervous.

The Queen took the Princess into her arms. "You look lovely, my dear," she said to her in Arabic.

"Oh Mother, are you sure that this is right?"

"Of course, sweet one. Come, take a look at her. She's beautiful."

The Queen guided the Princess over to where Fatima knelt, her arms still bound behind her. She gently took Fatima's face in her hands and turned it upwards so that the Princess could look into it.

"This girl is a creature of pleasure. She has been trained to give delight. She knows how to pleasure a woman. It's time you learned what fleshly pleasures a woman's body is capable of. Do not fear this girl. She will treat you gently and with loving care. She is yours for the night. Enjoy her." The Queen kissed her daughter and left the room.

Without understanding the words, Fatima understood exactly what was expected of her. She looked up at the shy, uncertain girl. The Princess was a desirable young woman. She had kind eyes. Her breasts were firm and ample enough for her slender frame. She had a pretty face, unmarked by avarice or cruelty. The French girl's loins stirred at that thought of the sweet caresses she could give her.

The lights in the room had been turned down low and there was a sweet smell of incense in the room. The Princess sat on the bed nervously contemplating the young girl who knelt beside her. Part of her yearned for the girl's embrace, and the other part wanted to call the whole thing off. This girl was vastly experienced at sex and she had none. Not even a kiss. The Princess was afraid that the girl would mock her innocence.

Suddenly, as if propelled to action, the Princess got up from the bed. She moved about the room lighting small votive candles. When she had finished, she turned off the lights.

The room was even dimmer now, and the Princess felt less uneasy about the task to come. For she saw it as a task, one compelled by her mother's wishes. Alliyah dreamed of a strong man's arms; like she had read of in the cheap romance novels she had stolen from her mother's room. She wanted to be overcome by a man's passion, possessed by him. She had never harbored a desire to make love to a woman. But her mother had said that she must and so she would, just this once, just to see what it was like.

Fatima had watched the young princess scurry nervously about the room. When the lights were extinguished she understood the Princess's need for the cover of darkness. She remembered when she was innocent, when she first yearned for a lover's touch. It had been a young boy in her school, a year ahead of her. They had made love at his house, when his parents were away. She was afraid to be seen naked, afraid to see a look of disappointment in the young boy's eyes. She had made him turn off all of the lights. Now her nakedness was for all to see.

When the Princess returned to the bed and resumed her sitting position, Fatima realized that she would have to take matters into her own hands. She did not want to make an enemy of the Queen by failing in her duty. She sensed a hard taskmaster in the Queen and remembered the hard slaps she had given her on the day of her arrival. She had been beaten almost senseless by Rashan, but she sensed that any punishment inflicted by the Queen would be infinitely more exquisite.

Fatima rose from her knees and turning her back to the Princess offered her her bound wrists. The Princess was startled by the slave girl's sudden movement, but she realized that she would have to untie the girl. Her hands, moist with sweat, and trepidation in her heart, she undid the leather thong.

Fatima's hands were free. She turned and looked the Princess in the eyes. The flickering candles made shadows dance across the Princess's face. Fatima sat next to her and reaching a hand up, gently stroked the other woman's cheek. The Princess drew back slightly, but allowed the caress. The hand was warm, almost hot. Alliyah trembled.

Encouraged by her boldness, Fatima leaned forwards slowly. With her hand still on the Princess's cheek, she drew her lips close to hers. She could feel the nervousness of the girl. Before placing her lips on the Princess's, she hesitated, looking for a sign of resistance or refusal. Seeing none, Fatima leaned forwards just a quarter inch more and the lips of the two girls met. It was a soft kiss, more like a caress. The Princess's lips were soft and sweet. Fatima felt a well of affection rise within her. She leaned back and smiled. The Princess's eyes looked downwards demurely and she smiled too.

The French girl now placed her other hand on the Princess's face and, holding her head steady, kissed her again, stronger now, bolder. She made small kisses around the outline of the Princess's mouth, along her chin and over her eyes. She drew her body closer. The two women could feel each other's warmth through their delicate clothes. Alliyah sighed, mesmerized by Fatima's eager lips. Fatima found the Princess's lips again and, after pressing them firmly with her own, gently guided the young girl's mouth open.

Alliyah inhaled the hot breath of the slave girl. She was feeling things that she never would have guessed at. Her nipples had grown firm, and there was an incipient yearning in her loins.

When Fatima's tongue touched hers, a soft, hesitant touch, Alliyah felt a flow of warmth through her body. All her thoughts were on the gentle tongue in her mouth and the hot, but sweet breath of the other girl. Unconsciously, her hands reached out for the body of the other, and she rested them on the slave girl's hips. Fatima delved deeper into Alliyah's mouth, her own passions rising.

For several minutes, the two young women explored each other's tongues. "So this is a kiss," Alliyah thought. "It's like the taste of a luscious fruit, better."

Fatima broke off the kiss and gently pushed the Princess's hands from her hips. With one motion, she pulled her teddy over her head, revealing her slender, curvaceous body. Her nipples had hardened with lust for her young mistress. Her breasts felt taut. She sensed the lubrication of her sex.

The Princess's eyes gorged themselves on Fatima's flesh. Shadows flickered over it as the light of the candles danced about. It seemed mysterious to her, exotic. It was like her own, but different. Alliyah felt the slave girl's hand take hold of her wrist and raise it to her breast. She watched, amazed as Fatima placed it on one of her soft, round orbs. The flesh was hot, yet supple. When Fatima released her wrist, she kept her hand in place, gently squeezing the heavy orb and then cupping it. Her eyes were fixated at the firm nipple and the circle of rough flesh around it. She felt Fatima's hand on the back of her head, gently pulling her forward. Startled at first, she looked into the slave's face. Seeing only the French girl's tender smile and soft, wet eyes, she allowed herself to be pulled closer to the delicate mound. She parted her lips and took the hard button of flesh into her mouth. She nearly swooned as she engulfed the breast's tip, sucking on it, tasting another's flesh for the first time.

Without the need for further encouragement, the Princess brought her body closer to Fatima's. She was holding both of Fatima's breasts now as she suckled passionately. She turned her oral caresses to the other breast and heard the slave girl moan. She answered with a moan of her own.

Again, Fatima gently pushed the Princess back. Standing next to the bed, she pulled Alliyah to her feet. They were about the same height and their eyes met. Fatima placed her hands on the Princess's neck and tenderly drew the shoulders of the sheer nightgown down her arms. Trembling, the Princess let the garment fall to the floor around her. She was naked. She had thought that the process of disrobing before this sensual, experienced young woman would be awkward and disconcerting. But the other girl's tender and appreciative gaze made her nudity seem natural. Fatima stepped forward and rubbed her taut nipples against Alliyah's. A jolt of electricity shot through the innocent girl. She felt the other girl's arms wrap around her and pull her closer. Their breasts and bellies were pressed together. The sensual melding of their flesh was overwhelming to Alliyah. She had never dreamed that sex would be like this. She circled her own arms around Fatima, pressing their bodies closer together, enjoying the sensuous warmth of Fatima's skin. Her virgin sex burned with desire. When she felt Fatima's lips on hers she opened her mouth hungrily. The two women were overcome by passion. Their mouths feasted on each other's, their hands seeking out soft and tender flesh.

The French girl slowly edged them back over to the bed. She guided her royal lover down and onto her back. Their lips were still joined as she lay her body next to Alliyah's and drew her hand across her breasts, down her stomach and to the throbbing lips below.

As Fatima placed her hand on Alliyah's sex, the Princess let out a long, low moan. She spread her legs wide to receive Fatima's caress. Fatima took one of Alliyah's teats in her mouth and bit down on it softly. Alliyah's moan turned into a soft cry. Her body felt strange, as if all of her cells had been awakened. Her breathing had become heavy, her pussy hot. Delicately, Fatima teased the hard nub of pleasure at the apex of Alliyah's wet gash. Alliyah was now rocking her hips, trying to grind her sex against the hand that tormented her. She could feel a surge of pleasure as her pussy throbbed. A wave of delight passed through her body. Her arms clutched Fatima closer. She sought out her lover's lips. As their tongues merged once more, Alliyah's passion was released. Wave after of wave of intense pleasure flowed through her as her pussy pulsed and throbbed. She began to cry out, "Oh! Oh! Oh!" as she came for the first time in someone's arms.

Fatima had been pressing her pussy down on Alliyah's thigh, rubbing her clit against the hot tight skin. When she felt the throes of passion flow through Alliyah, her own orgasm was sparked. She grabbed the moist nether lips of the girl beneath her, and pressed her thighs vise-like around Alliyah's leg. She shuddered as her whole body received her cunt's blessing.

When their orgasms had subsided, the two women lay in each other's arms, dazed and contented. Their bodies were covered with perspiration, their skin glistening in the candlelight. Overcome with happiness and delight, Alliyah began to cry.

Twice more that night, the two women made passionate love to each other. Alliyah could not get enough of Fatima's flesh. She rolled on top of the young girl and held her hands tightly over her head. She drove her tongue into Fatima's mouth and pressed their sexes together. It seemed natural for her to be rubbing her clit on the French girl's. Fatima was a delicious fountain of pleasure at which she yearned to drink. She learned to fondle Fatima's sex, learned to crave the pungent aroma of her moist slit.

When the girls had exhausted their forces, they just lay there holding each other, gently caressing each other's bodies. They were both experiencing a dream-like state, but of quite different varieties. Fatima dreamed of being the master of her own fate, of living free, loving whom she wished. Alliyah dreamed of a life of sensual pleasure, of keeping this warm sensuous lover for her own.

Unfortunately, neither dream could come true. The women had fallen asleep in each other's arms when, just before dawn, the Queen entered the room. She looked with knowing delight at the intertwined women. The slave girl had done her work well, that is as it should be. Now she must return to the harem, for she was the property of her son.

The Queen shook Fatima awake. The girl woke up suddenly, afraid, uncertain of where she was. When she saw the Queen, she knew that her idyll with the Princess had come to an end. She was a slave girl once more. A well of protest rose within her. But fear ruled her. Obediently, she slipped from the bed and fell to her knees before her mistress. The Queen stepped behind her and affixed her wrists together. As she was doing so, the Princess awoke. She was surprised to find herself alone in her bed. When she saw the French girl being bound, she felt sorrow. Her lover was a chattel owned by her brother. She had heard the stories of his cruelty. Her heart went out to the abject slave girl.

"Mother," she whispered, not wanting to disturb the dreamlike atmosphere of the room. "Please don't take her back, not yet."

"She must go back, Alliyah, she is a slave, not a person. Don't forget that."

"Can I kiss her, please, just one more time?" Alliyah begged.

"Of course," the Queen replied, knowing the tender passion that introduction into the world of physical pleasure could bring.

Alliyah stood and pulled Fatima to her feet. The slave girl stood, her eyes downcast, afraid to look at the

Princess in the presence of the Queen. Alliyah lifted her chin and kissed her lightly on the lips. In English she said to the abject girl, "Thank you." It was the only words she spoke to her all night. She turned to her mother, "Will I see her again, Mother? Can she come to me again?"

"We'll see," the Queen responded curtly.

The Queen quickly hooded Fatima and clicked a leash to her collar. She patted her daughter on the head and urged her to go back to sleep. She then towed Fatima from the room.

CHAPTER SIXTEEN

A GIRL IS PUNISHED

Tulip's limbs encircled me as we rested after our passionate bout. After ten minutes of motionless silence, the telephone rang. I jumped at its discordant tone. The phone was beside the bed on a small, white table and I answered it. "Wiggins," I said. It was Anthony.

"Harry, wake up. Let's play!"

"Okay, okay," I mumbled, not really happy at his disturbance of my post-coital tranquility. "I'll be out in a minute."

I rose quickly from the bed and grabbed my robe. My sex hung heavy with the effects of the workout it had received so far this day. I looked back at Tulip who had also risen and was standing by the foot of the bed, her hands behind her back, her head lowered. I stepped up to her, raised her chin and kissed her plump lips. "I'll be back later," I told her.

She smiled and whispered, "Thank you, master."

When I stepped out to the patio that sat outside the supervisor's dormitory, Anthony was waiting for me. The sunlight had dimmed since my siesta and a cool breeze again ran across the plateau on which the resort sat.

"I want you to meet a couple of the other supervisors. You may get a chance to work with them,"

Anthony told me.

We walked along the brick pathway until we reached a building that served as a restaurant and night club. There was a large outdoor dining area, which was filled with robes of blue and brown. As we approached I could see, amongst the laughing and merry men, naked women dashing to and fro carrying trays of food, drinks and other odds and ends. There was not a one who could not have graced the cover of a fashion magazine. "Where do they get all of these beautiful women?" I asked myself. "Are there any left back in the world?"

Anthony led me over to a table at which sat two brown robed men. One was a tall, lanky fellow, dark of brow. I could see that his physique was tightly packed, belying his thin frame. He had a cruel face, hard eyes. The other fellow was Latino, shorter than the first fellow. There was a large scar down his right cheek. Looking at him, you got the sense that he wore it as some kind of trophy. The scar was partially obscured by a scruffy beard. As he rose to acknowledge Anthony's introduction of me, I saw his natural, cat like grace. He smiled as he shook my hand, a gold tooth sparkling in his mouth.

"Harry," Anthony addressed me, "I'd like you to meet Thorndike and Cholo. They've worked for the company for a quite a long time."

I shook first Cholo's hand and then Thorndike's. While Cholo's face registered a modicum of amiability, Thorndike scowled. I concluded that he was not a social animal.

"Fellows," Anthony continued, "this is Harry. He's

just joined us yesterday. May we sit down?"

I don't know what Anthony would have said if the guy Thorndike had said no. My guess was that Anthony had some real pull around here which he probably earned by not letting many guys say no to him. Also, when you've got the world by the cunt hairs, so to speak, why mess it up by being ornery. I remembered what Anthony had said about body bags off the back of cabin cruisers. Why die when you were already in heaven?

Thorndike nodded a reluctant consent. Cholo was more munificent.

"Sure," he said with a wide grin. "Sit down. I'm always glad to meet a friend of Anthony's."

Anthony and I sat down. "So what's your story, Harry," Cholo asked.

"My story?" I replied. "I'm just a bad boy who's stepped in shit."

Cholo laughed.

A daintily bosomed, blond haired girl came up to us. She looked about 5'4" and had her hair in a page boy cut. There was a little red ribbon tied to her collar. "May I be of service, masters?" she asked, her head bowing slightly. She carried a small tray with a little pad on it. Her thighs were slim, her hips just a hint short of wide. She wore bright red lipstick, which was matched by polish on her fingernails and toes. Tiny silver bells hung from her nipples.

"Harry?" Anthony queried me.

"A Bombay martini, straight up with a twist of lemon," I ordered.

Anthony ordered a Johnny Walker red and soda.

When the girl walked away, I asked him what the red ribbon was for.

"When a slave is wearing a red ribbon it means that they can be claimed for the night. It has their number on it. These girls get off duty at 8 o'clock. If a girl is claimed, they will be chained to the wall in the main lounge. You just present the ribbon and she's yours."

"Nice," I commented. I looked around and most of the girls still wore their red ribbons. A tall black man dressed in a starched pure white tee shirt and matching pants and shoes came over to our table. He wordlessly passed menus to Anthony and me and walked away.

Anthony explained. "The girls only take drink orders. Anything more complicated, like a meal, is taken by one of the servants. The girls do all the hauling, but he takes the order."

I picked out a nice sounding veal dish while Anthony ordered fish. Thorndike and Cholo had apparently just finished their meals and our waitress, after she delivered our drinks, removed their plates.

Cholo eyed the girl lustfully. "Hey, cunt," he called out.

The girl turned around and faced Cholo, her head bowed as before.

"When you're done with that stuff, come right back, you hear?"

"As you wish, master," she replied and scurried away.

I took a sip of my chilled, ass kicking martini. I felt a flow of warmth through my body. It sure beat jail house gin. The girl was back before I put my glass down. She immediately fell to her knees next to Cholo's chair. She crossed her hands behind her back and bowed her head.

"Get up, slut," Cholo told her. Slowly, she rose to her feet.

"Let me see those tiny little tits of yours, slut," he ordered.

The girl stepped up to Cholo and presented her breasts to him. He grabbed both nipples in his hands and twisted them harshly. The girl grimaced, but made no protest.

"Are you a good fuck, slut?" Cholo asked her.

"Yes master," the girl responded, flatly. She had a slight accent to her English. I wasn't sure, but I thought that she might be Scandinavian.

"Do you like it up the ass, slut?" Cholo inquired, his voice cold and harsh. He was not taking a poll.

"If it pleases the master," the girl said, timidly. Cholo still held her nipples twisted tightly in his fingers. I could see the girl's obvious discomfort, although she tried not to show it. The Latino released her tits.

"Turn around," Chino ordered churlishly. The girl took a little spin on her heels. All the serving girls wore bright red 'fuck me' high heels. "It must be the devil to scoot around on those things," I thought. Cholo ran his hand over her ass. It was rounded and full. "An ass made for whipping, slut. Do you like to be whipped, slut?" he asked her.

I could see the girl stiffen. Cholo's question carried more than a hint of menace. I sensed that he was not an amateur when it came to a whip and that his inquiry was not of an academic nature.

"If it pleases the master," she said in a tremulous voice. I guessed that a whipping was something that you really never got used to. This girl was probably cursing her luck that she had been assigned to our table. On the other hand, if she had any luck, she wouldn't be here at all.

"Get down on your knees and let me see you stroke your cunt," Cholo ordered. "I want to see you get off. And, you better not fake it, slut."

The girl dropped instantly to her knees. She spread them wide and, spreading her labial lips apart with one hand, began to massage her clit with the other. She placed her index finger on the little button of pleasure there and slowly rubbed her clit in a circular motion. The heel of her hand rested on a small tuft of blond hair above her pussy. She closed her eyes, taking herself away to who knows where. I wondered where she could take her mind to to drive out the harsh reality of her surroundings. She looked to be about 22 or 23 years old. Her face looked peaceful with her eyes closed. I guessed that even an abject sexual slave had some reminiscences of good times. Was she imagining some past lover, a boyfriend from her younger days? Or did she construct some imaginary being who tenderly worshiped her delightful flesh?

Whatever the case, I soon saw that the girl's efforts were bearing fruit. Her slit glistened with moisture. She was kneeling next to me, facing Cholo who was to my right. Her legs were spread wide enough so that her engorged nether lips and the crevasse between them were clearly visible to me. Her small breasts had grown firm and hard, her chest was reddening, a sign of her developing passion. The girl had parted her ruby red lips and had begun to breathe deeply.

I was interrupted briefly by the other waitress who had brought my veal. When I looked back, the girl was leaning back on one hand, her back arched. Her hand had spread the moisture from her pussy all over her mons and she was delving deeply inside herself with her red tipped fingers. The room around us had grown silent as men became drawn to the girl's lascivious display. I downed the rest of my martini in one gulp. I didn't know about anyone else, but the girl's efforts had produced a hardness in my already well used cock. I noticed more than one man with his hand in his robe.

The girl's lust began to rise and she commenced a low, guttural moan. She started to rub her pussy faster and faster. When her orgasm's convulsions commenced, she opened her eyes suddenly, only to have them roll back as the waves of passion overcame her. She uttered one, long, languid cry and was done. There was a loud and appreciative round of applause.

She took a moment to catch her breath and then she looked up at Cholo timidly, seeking approval from the only man that mattered right now. God help her if he was dissatisfied.

Cholo was intent on the girl. "Get up and bring me your cunt, whore," he said. She rose gracefully from the floor and presented her loins to her master. She was standing right next to me, her legs spread wide to give Cholo access to her moist, soft pussy and I could see the sheen of sweat that covered her from her exertions, little rivulets descending from her armpits, a tiny drop hanging from the stiff nipple of one breast. Her face was flushed, her lips pouty. She was still breathing heavily. I could smell the tell-tale odor of her juices. Cholo put his hand on her sex and probed it callously. He lifted his hand to his nose and took a deep breath, savoring the aroma.

"You're a good little whore, slut," he told her. He reached out his hand and took the red ribbon from her collar, disappointing about thirty other guys, including me. "Tonight I will beat you and then you will suck me off, whore. Is that all right with you?"

The girl trembled at Cholo's promise. There was no doubt in my mind that he would carry it out. With a tremulous voice, so low so that it could hardly be heard amid the resumed cacophony of the dining room, she said, "As the master pleases."

Following a dismissive nod of Cholo's head, the girl retreated into the safety of the crowded dining area. Cholo looked over at Thorndike and the two men laughed. I had not yet begun my meal and was trying to regain my equilibrium. I wanted another drink.

"You've scared our waitress away," I jokingly told Cholo.

"Hey, there's a hundred more where she came from," Cholo said. "How'd you like the show?" he asked me.

"Well, it's no way to treat a lady," I answered, "but who am I to say?

Thorndike spoke for the first time. His voice was low and gravelly. "There are no ladies on this island, Harry, don't you know that? Just cunts."

"Thanks for the information," I answered, not sure if Thorndike was trying to get under my skin. Out of prison habit I noted the sharp knife on the table next to my plate. Anthony must have seen me tense up. In prison, especially a Federal max like Atlanta, you didn't take shit from nobody unless you wanted to be somebody's fuck toy.

"Relax, Harry," he said. "Thorndike's just being friendly. Anthony looked at Thorndike with a commanding glance. "Aren't you?" he asked him.

Thorndike paused. I didn't like anyone to have to intercede for me in a beef and I sensed that Thorndike was measuring me. He smiled after a moment and took a gulp of his white wine that was in front of him. "Yeah," he said. "Informative."

I slowly passed a bite of veal into my mouth. "Thanks," I said, shooting back Thorndike's icy glare.

The meal passed without too much more exchange between us. A waitress brought Thorndike and Cholo coffee and me another martini. I felt a drunk coming on.

When the buxom, auburn haired waitress had delivered my refreshment withdrew, Anthony tried to start up some cordial conversation between us.

"Harry's lined up to do some enforcement work for us. He was doing a lifer for murder one until a couple of days ago. He used to work for Tony B. He comes highly recommended."

A noted a slight look of respect from Thorndike. My pedigree established, he seemed to relax. Cholo spoke up.

"I know Tony B. I used to run cars for him out of Philly down to the ports. I did my first stretch working for him. Eighteen months in Harrisburg."

"That's the guy," I said, swallowing down a mouthful of the delicious veal. I was going to get fat here.

Thorndike spoke next. "How do you feel about our little enterprise here, Harry? Not too outré for you, is it?"

"Whatever Mr. Klitzman wants from me, he gets," I replied. There was silence around the table. I sensed I had committed a faux pas.

"We don't mention our employer's name in public, Harry" Anthony told me.

"Oh," I answered stupidly. "My bad."

Thorndike rose from his chair, finished with his meal. "We have an excellent gym here, Harry," he said to me as he pushed in his chair. "It has a boxing ring. Care to go a few rounds with me tomorrow? Have a little fun?"

I thought I might enjoy bending this guy's nose back a bit. "Okay, Thorndike. Afternoon o.k.?"

"Afternoon it is," he replied. "See you, Anthony," he said, nodding to my escort.

"I'll come and watch," Anthony answered.

The two men sauntered from the restaurant. I could see them laughing and talking as they walked down the brick pathway that led to the lounges. "Somewhere out there is a piece of tail that's going to be sorry she got up this morning," I thought. I could just imagine what cruelties Thorndike might inflict on a girl.

"Harry," Anthony said, finishing off the last piece of his fish, "Thorndike is mighty handy with the gloves. I've seen him take guys apart. Are you up for this?"

I knew that I couldn't back down. "I'm up for it," I

replied with a sinking feeling in my gut. If Anthony had to mention how good Thorndike was, he must be pretty good. My longest fight was a one rounder in a strip joint in Hackensack. I threw three punches and then hit the guy with a beer bottle. Most fights I had been in were two punch jobs. You hit the other guy first and then hit him again as he goes down. I decided to worry about that tomorrow.

"So what's this guy Thorndike do?" I asked Anthony.

"He's a procurer. You know, he collects product for us. Women."

"A kidnapper?"

"No," Anthony replied. "He's more of a woman stealer. What he takes he never gives back. He runs a couple of crews. They come in to an area, do a few set ups. Thorndike comes in, gives the raw material the once over and okays the snatch. He's got a good eye for cunt."

"He looks pretty mean to me," I observed.

"Yeah," Anthony said. "But not meaner than Cholo. I watched him skin a guy once. It took three hours. I never saw so much blood."

"What did the guy do to deserve that?" I asked, shocked.

Anthony shrugged as he mopped up the sauce from his plate with a piece of roll. "I don't know. I think he owed us money or something."

I wondered what they did to guys who ratted them out. I began to wonder whether my little gamble was worth the tearing off of strips of my skin, bit by bit until I was a raw piece of meat. I shivered, involuntarily.

The buxom girl came up and took our plates. She came back with coffee and a tray of mints. I admired the sway of her large, firm breasts as she leaned over to put the tray on the table. I couldn't resist seizing the breast nearest me and squeezing it gently. The girl curtsied slightly and looked up at me with a slight smile.

"Is there anything the master wants?" she said invitingly. I was nonplussed by the candor of her invitation.

"Not today," I replied. I felt stupid. Anthony waved her away. He smiled at me.

"What's the matter, Harry, too much for you?"

I looked over at him sheepishly. "I just didn't expect such enthusiasm for her work," I said. "A happy slave?"

"You'll find that there are all kinds of reactions women have to sexual slavery, Harry," Anthony instructed me. "Some, like the young slut there, learn to adjust to a life of fucking and sucking. I'll bet that girl's come three or four times already today. When she sees a hunk of a newcomer like you, well, she can't resist it."

"You mean she spotted me as new?"

"Almost certainly, Harry. You still have that little boy in the candy store look. You'll get past it in a few days."

"And what about the other women. How do they react?"

"Some never get used to it, like our little blond girl from before. Cholo spotted it right away. She'll be begging and pleading for mercy tonight and probably just about every night that she stays here. She'll probably go off to one of our Middle Eastern bordellos.

She'll have to be kept under lock and key all the time.

"And then there's everything in between. Some girls get to tolerate it. Like Adriana. I always get the sense that she's somewhere else when I fuck her. But her body's always right there. No complaints from me. Then there's the ones who just don't measure up. You know, can't get past being a sex slave. Most of them, and there aren't many, get dumped."

I assumed he meant off the back of an outboard. The visual image of a struggling form encased in a weighted body bag came to mind. I shivered again.

"You cold, Harry?" Anthony asked.

"No, just still a little squeamish," I answered. "I've never iced a woman."

"That's just the thing, Harry," Anthony told me. His voice was stern. I knew I was getting gospel. "You've got to stop thinking of them as women. Once they're bagged, they're not women anymore. They're delivery systems. They deliver sexual pleasure. Like any other thing, if they don't work, they get thrown away. And like some gizmos, if they're not working right, sometimes you gotta give them a little kick."

I pondered Anthony's cruel assessment of the future of the many beautiful, young naked creatures I had seen so far. I thought of the frightened Tulip back in my room, the graceful, but distant Adriana. When they stopped working right, they would be thrown away.

I finished my coffee and pushed my chair from the table. "What now?" I asked.

"I thought you would want to watch while I disciplined that slave from this morning," he said.

I had forgotten about the tender, delicate girl who

had dared to disobey Man Mountain Dean. I had, against my better nature, if I had one that is, been unexpectedly entranced by the beatings administered to Lois and Delia earlier that day. I had no reason to reject Anthony's proffer of another display of callous brutality. In fact, I had every reason not to. If I didn't fit in here and accept the twisted morality of the place, I was doomed. The girl would be whipped whether I watched or not.

"Sure, thanks," I said. "Where is she?"

"Oh, she's been waiting for us. Come on, she's on the other side of the compound."

We walked past several lowly built, white stoned buildings. Men and women had emerged from their mid-day torpor and the patios and verandas outside the buildings were full of people. We passed what looked like an outdoor café where naked and collared waitresses were serving colored tropical drinks with little umbrellas on them. Men's laughter and loud conversation filled the air. The women all were naked and silent, either kneeling at the foot of a master, or shuttling to and fro with trays of drinks and food.

We rounded the corner of a building and I saw a large concrete pad. On the pad were approximately ten waist high poles with tubes of steel welded to them horizontally. The poles were of two parts, a thick round tube of dull steel and a smaller one atop it telescoping in. This made the level of the horizontal tubes adjustable.

I saw draped over one of the tubes a woman's body. All that could be seen of her was her twin rear globes. The rest was covered by a black tarpaulin. Anthony strode up to the girl and pulled the tarpaulin off of her.

It was the girl from this morning all right. At least it looked like her. I had seen so many naked women that day that their faces and bodies had begun to mingle. The girl's midsection was bisected by the horizontal tube. Her wrists were affixed to rings at the bottom of the vertical pole as were her ankles. Her hair hung down, scraping the ground. A strap ran through the horizontal tube and across her back, holding her torso in place. She had been immobilized in a virtually folded position, half of her body on one side of the pole and the rest on the other, as if she were touching her toes. He ass stood out prominently, pointed upwards.

The skin on her rear was tinted a bright pink. She had obviously been left in the sun to bake while it had been at its worst. Anthony ran his hand over it and the girl stiffened. It looked tender as hell.

"After a while, Harry," Anthony addressed me, "a regular whipping just isn't enough. This cunt has been on report three times this month. That's something we just can't tolerate. So we have this special punishment for her."

The girl was gagged and so she protested with a mere whimper when Anthony slapped her right rear cheek. The outline of his hand, a white imprint, appeared where he had struck her and then faded quickly back to red. He stepped over to a wooden cabinet mounted on the rear wall of the building and brought out a long, thin reed. It was supple but strong. He swung it through the air experimentally, causing a deep 'whoosh'.

I looked over at the pinioned girl. Although

irremediably fastened in place, she was nervously shifting her feet, pulling at her restraints. A long, shrill desperate whine escaped her gag. She undoubtedly was aware of the exquisite pain she was about to endure.

Anthony reared his hand back and struck the girl across her rear with the reed. It gave a loud 'crack' as it landed on her flesh. A momentary line of white emerged amongst the pinkish display on the woman's ass, which turned immediately a bright red. In spite of the gag, I could hear the woman's screech of pain. Her body jumped in protest of its abuse. Anthony laughed. "See?" he said.

Five times Anthony struck the girl's rear globes with the reed. Each time a long red wound appeared and the girl protested wildly at her treatment. By the fifth blow, her rear and legs were shivering with pain. She was sobbing uncontrollably.

Anthony put away the reed. His excitement was obvious as his robe was tented. Mine was too. The scene of a naked, helpless woman being beaten was urgently compelling. I had watched while her buttocks danced to the lash. Her vuvla was displayed clearly between her thighs as there was an inch or two gap between them. Anthony now reached under the scarred posterior and stroked the hairless pudenda. After a short while, he raised his hand. His fingers were covered by the girl's lubrication. He showed it to me and smiled. "You're the guest, Harry. Want to go first?"

I was rock hard despite my lustful bout with the Tulip. Part of me protested against the harsh treatment of this poor girl. The other wanted to bury my cock in her moist hole. Guess which one won.

I pulled open my robe and stepped up to the girl's behind. Her pussy was at precisely the right level for my penetration. For a moment I hesitated at putting my hands on her abused flesh; even the side of her buttocks were covered in an angry pink. But there was no other way to gain sufficient purchase to impale the helpless and still moaning woman on my cock. I grabbed her hips and pushed the head of my cock towards the tantalizing, glistening lips. Her moans became louder as my hands tormented her sunburned flesh. I pushed inside her, my cock gliding effortlessly into her sheath.

As I started to pump my cock into her hot pussy, I looked up. We were facing the west side of the island and the sun was just beginning to set. The sky was covered with a fiery red glow interspersed with swirls of bright yellow. Since the club was situate on a plateau, with steep cliffs surrounding it, I could see the reflection of the yellow-orange ball and its colorful radiation on the wide expanse of ocean that lay before me. It was an amazing sight under any circumstances, but was made especially so with my cock sunk deep into a woman's body. My physical pleasure was enhanced by my visual delight. I had experienced amazing things that day, things I had never imagined to see. But this was the coup de jour, the topper.

My pleasure intensified as my juices began to rise. I was humping the girl rapidly, she, giving out little moans as I struck her buttocks with my hips. I was grabbing her hips tightly as I rammed my cock in as far as it would go. I could feel the heat given off by her sunburned flesh. When my cock began to throb and spill my seed into her womb, my eyes rolled back and my knees got weak. I was mindless of the spectacle I made, humping this forlorn girl in the presence of that beautiful sky and under the eyes of my erstwhile Virgil, who had been leading me through the various levels of this earthly purgatory.

When I had done, I withdrew my manhood. It was sloppy with her juices and mine. Anthony was grinning at me, almost stupidly. "You see why we do it here?" he said. "Nothing like it, eh?"

I nodded and stepped back to allow him to take his pleasure. I watched mesmerized as he stroked his piece into the girl. He punctuated his motion by a few loud slaps on the girl's ass. She whined and groaned in response.

The tendrils of the sunset spread wildly across the sky. Its reflection, disturbed slightly by the almost tranquil water, was a surreal cacophony of colors. Anthony was right, prison was never like this.

CHAPTER SEVENTEEN

FATE TAKES A HAND

When the Prince returned from his trip, he celebrated with a long night of abuse of his slave. Fatima had been counting the days and she knew on the morning of the eleventh day that she was doomed to see the Prince that night. She spent the day morosely haunting the harem, so much so that the other girls, with the sole exception of her lover Gelela, unconsciously shunned her. When Ngomo called her name after dinner, she ran fearfully to his feet. When she was bound and hooded, she began to pray nervously to herself.

The Prince had not yet arrived in his boudoir when Ngomo led the frightened and despondent girl inside. He leashed her to the bedpost and guided her to her knees. He felt sorry for this little one. It went against his grain to see a beautiful creature like this slowly, but surely, destroyed, long before her time. He knew that most of the slave girls were destined for unsavory fates. That was the natural progression of things. Unless they were lucky enough to capture the heart of a master, they would eventually be sold, and, as they aged or showed signs of wear, they would descend the ladder until they were little more than street whores, sucking cocks for harsh tavern owners or lodged in some dismal brothel. When no one wanted them, they would, if they were lucky, be given a quiet death.

But this one would not last so long. Already he could see that he spirit was flagging. Ngomo had learned in his many years of service to the Emir that even slaves needed a sense of appreciation, of value. This slave was treated meaner than the vilest dog.

Fatima knelt at her station for two hours, hours that were a literal hell. Her heart began to pound each time she thought she heard the opening of the door. When she finally heard the door open, her heart sank. It was time.

The Prince, of course was drunk. He saw his property chained to his bed and rejoiced. He had missed abusing this little bitch, he thought. Tonight, he would make up for it.

Knocking back another large shot of scotch whiskey, the Prince considered how he would use his little whore; he would give her a good fucking, of course. But first she must be reminded of the power that he wielded over her. She would be punished for the very act of stirring his loins.

The Prince removed his clothing and tossed them in a corner of the room. He tore off the black silk bag that covered her head and undid her chain. He pulled his slave to her feet by her hair, causing her to give a little cry. "Did you miss me slut?" he taunted her in English. "Did you miss my stiff cock?" He grabbed her cheeks with his hand. "Or was it the whip that you missed, eh?"

The girl was frantic in her fear. The Prince was meanest when he was drunk, and he was clearly well into his cups. She had learned a smattering of English now from the girls in the harem. She knew what a slut was, that he was calling her a whore. She knew the word 'whip', too. As the Prince relaxed his grip on her face, she managed to eke out one of the phrases in English that she had been taught.

"May I pleasure you cock, Master?"

The Prince was surprised. He had never heard her speak except to beg him, mostly in French, to grant her surcease from his punishments. He laughed.

"Yes, you can suck my cock, whore. That's what you're here for. But first I think we'll have a little fun."

He spun the girl around and untied her hands. "Take off that rag," he commanded her.

Fatima caught the gist of his demand and quickly pulled off the golden, lace trimmed teddy that she had worn. When she had cast it on the floor, the Prince dragged her onto the bed. At first she thought that he was acceding to her request. If she could keep him sexually excited, maybe he would neglect to beat her. After a second orgasm, he might pass out. But she had misread her master's intent.

The Prince stepped over to a cabinet, one that Fatima knew very well. She knew what was in it because she had seen him draw from it the various instruments of her torture on many occasions. She watched with trepidation as she saw him draw three long lengths of soft, cotton rope from the cabinet and then return to the bed. She watched disconsolately as he tied a rope to each of her ankles. She was sitting on the bed, her legs splayed wide, her hands behind her for support. The Prince pushed her to her back and, grabbing her hands, secured them in front of her with one end of a rope. He drew the other end to the head of the bed and affixed it there, pulling the girl's arms taut above her head.

He leaned over her, rubbing his hand over her breasts and belly. He could feel her trembling. She should be frightened, he thought, as he stared into her widened eyes. "What should I whip, my little harlot?" he said. "Should I whip these lovely tits?" His face was close to hers; she could feel his whisky laden breath. His black eyes peered into hers as his hand found her soft mound between her legs. He pinched the twin lips together harshly.

"Or should it be your precious quim?" He twisted the lips hard, causing Fatima to emit a groan of pain.

She wished that she had the courage to defy him, to spit in his face. He could whip her until she died then, she wouldn't care. But she loathed the pain that he inflicted. That they all had inflicted on her. It's repetition during her training had broken her will to resist it.

The fact that she had been forced to endure the unendurable had not hardened her, it had made her more afraid, less tolerant of pain. She hated to be lashed, but she knew that there were more severe forms of torture. And, she wanted to live. She had not given up all hope of the resumption of freedom. Someday, somehow, she would escape. She held on to this intently as a shipwrecked sailor would hold on to the last bit of wreckage that kept him afloat.

So rather than spit into this evil man's face, the French girl retreated into herself. She closed her eyes and turned her head away from her tormentor. He could do what he wanted. She would endure; she would survive.

The Prince was enraged by his victim's passivity. He lashed out and slapped her across the breasts, violently and repeatedly. The French girl was startled by the vehemence of his reaction. The iron hands of the Prince insulted her flesh. Stinging pain coursed through her. She began to cry out, "Oh! Oh! Oh!" as her breasts were flung wildly back and forth as a result of the blows.

'Crack! Crack! Crack!' The repeated blows echoed throughout the room. 'Crack! Crack! Crack!' The Prince struck her tender breasts again and again with his open hand.

"You cunt!" he yelled. "You don't turn your face from me! You'll take your punishment and like it, you whore!"

'Crack! Crack! Crack!'

The suffering girl had tried to twist her body away from the blows, but the Prince had sat himself on her thighs. With her hands tied above her, the poor girl's breasts were easy targets for the Prince's wrath.

Something burst in the French girl. She lost all sense of where she was, of what she was. Her anger welled up in her like it never had before. "Ohhhhhhhh!" she cried out. "You pig, you fucking bastard!" she yelled in French. And then, in quite clear English, she yelled, "Fuck you! Fuck You!"

The Prince saw red. He slapped her hard in the face, drawing blood from her lip. He slapped her again and again. "What did you say, you fucking cunt!" he yelled. "I'll teach you to swear at me!"

He jumped off of the girl and ran to the cabinet by the wall. Grabbing a leather gag, he ran back and jumped back onto the bed. The French girl was horrified at what she had done. She knew that she would suffer tonight as she had never suffered before. She begged him in French, "No, no, please! I'm sorry! I'm sorry!"

The Prince could not see past his rage to observe her remorse for what she had done. He would not have cared if he did. He threw his leg over her and regained his perch atop her thighs.

"You're going to be sorry you ever said anything like that to me you cunt'" he growled at her.

Fatima tried to shrink away from the enraged Prince. She whimpered, "I'm sorry. I'm sorry. I'm sorry," over and over again. She grimaced as he presented the long thick leather plug of the gag to her face. He grabbed her face, pressing hard with his vise-like grip.

"Open you're fucking mouth, you worthless slut!" he ordered. His eyes were wild with wrath; his face had turned red with his rage. "Open your fucking mouth!" he screamed.

Reluctantly, Fatima opened her mouth. Tears were rolling down her face like a stream. His grip on her face was painful. As her lips parted, the Prince jammed the gag into her mouth. The end of the plug struck the back of her mouth painfully. He mashed the gag onto her face.

"Those are the last words you're ever going to speak, you cunt!" he told her as he pressed down with all of his weight. "You are going to wear this gag night and day until you die! The only time you'll have it out will be when I want to shove my dick down your throat!"

Fatima tried to shake her head, 'no', but the Prince's fierce grip of her face held it still. He pulled her head up by her hair and fastened the straps of the gag behind her head. Satisfied that she was effectively silenced, the Prince swung his legs off of her and came around to the foot of the bed. He grabbed the rope affixed to one ankle and tossed it over the rail of the canopy on one side. He pulled on it harshly and Fatima's left leg was yanked into the air. The girl watched him with terror as he tied off the end. He then did the same with her right leg.

Fatima's legs were splayed wide, exposing the plump hairless mound between them. Her ass was several inches in the air. Her hands were held taut above her. The only movement she could muster was to swing her hips from side to side, as she struggled, wild with fear.

The Prince drew from his cabinet a long, thin switch made of hickory wood. It narrowed from the handle to its tip, which was perhaps a centimeter wide. He swished it through the air appreciatively. "This will do nicely," he thought.

He approached the sorrowful woman. She could see him between her legs, his face taut with cruel determination. He had beaten her many times before. But that had been for his amusement, the joy he felt in inflicting pain on a helpless victim. This time he was motivated by a specific desire to inflict pain as retribution, retribution for daring to protest his callous abuse.

The Prince paused. The girl's thighs were pale as cream, soft as silk. He had not beaten her there yet. Not the insides of the thighs. It was almost as if he had been saving it for a night like this. "Are you ready, cunt?" he called to the French girl. She pleaded desperately with her eyes. The Prince reared back his arm.

'Swish. Crack!' The first blow fell on Fatima's right inner thigh, about four inches below the joining place of the thigh and the hip. A bright red line appeared where the switch had met the girl's flesh. Fatima convulsed in pain. She bit hard down on the gag between her teeth, suppressing her scream.

'Swish! Crack!' The Prince, using his left hand had struck the inside of the French girl's left thigh. Another angry red line appeared. Again the French girl's body tensed as it absorbed the painful lash. Again she bit down on the gag with all of her might. When the third blow stuck, directly atop her proffered cunt, she could bear no more. She screamed wildly, her hips rocked. Her breasts danced on her chest as she writhed in pain. The sound of her scream was muffled by the leather plug in her mouth, but it could not suppress all of the high pitched wail.

Rashan was pleased. He had struck gold. He brought the whip down three more times on the girl's tender sex. Each time the French girl screamed louder and louder. Methodically, he worked his way up one thigh and down the other. Repeatedly the slender whip sliced into the girl's skin. Fatima emitted a continuous, pitiful wail as she suffered again and again.

The wrathful nobleman paused to admire his

handiwork. Fatima's thighs and pussy were a latticework of red lines. In places, small drops of blood oozed from her wounds. Fatima's wailing slowed as the continuous application of the whip had ceased. She looked up, hopeful that the Prince's bloodlust had been sated. She saw from his eyes that it had not.

"I think we can move on, cunt," the Prince spat out at her. "How about those pretty tits? Are you ready for some more? I haven't even started yet!" he exclaimed.

He moved to the side of the bed where he had an unobstructed view of his next target. Fatima's chest was rising and falling rapidly, her body trying to recover the energy she had expended during her paroxysms of pain. The movement of her chest caused her pale white mounds to shiver invitingly. The Prince leaned over the terrified girl. He rested his lash on the bed. "What a pretty pair of tits," he said tauntingly. "So inviting." He placed his hands atop them, squeezing them gently.

Fatima was revolted by his touch, but hoping against hope that she could use the currency of her body to deter this madman, she repressed her reaction. The Prince leaned over and placed his lips on a nipple, sucking on it, enjoying its hardness. He placed his lips, then, on the other, reveling in its tactile surface. He looked up, into Fatima's desperately hopeful eyes. "Pretty little titties," he said in a child-like voice. He squeezed them again, harder this time until he saw the girl wince. "I'm going to whip these pretty little titties until they bleed."

He rose from the bed. His cock was rampant, his lust enraged. He grabbed the bottle of scotch from the credenza and drank directly from it, hungrily. He wiped his lips with his arm and glared at his captive. Wordlessly, he picked up the hickory reed and positioned himself alongside the girl. She closed her eyes and winced, a fruitless effort to gird herself for the blow.

'Swish! Crack!' The reed struck across the tops of Fatima's breasts. She moaned loudly with pain. It was if a terrible beast had ripped its claw across her tender globes. A telltale line of red appeared. As before, the Prince methodically inflicted blow after blow onto his targets. He crossed to the other side of the bed to achieve parity between the injuries to the breasts. Fatima rocked and shook, screaming woefully into her gag. Finally, after the twin, pale mounds had been crisscrossed with over a dozen angry lines of red, the Prince's ire was partially sated, enough, that is, for his lust to rise to preeminence. Fatima sobbed and sobbed, tears streaming down her face. She cursed herself for being born.

The Prince threw down the lash and crawled onto the bed. His object was the cruelly distended mouth that had offended him. He tore off the gag and slapped the girl's face twice. "You're going to take my cock down your throat, whore. If you so much as nick my cock, I'll have you flayed alive. Do you know what that means, slut?" he asked her. Fatima stared at him, her brow furled, waiting to hear what could possibly be worse than the merciless beating she had just received.

The Prince's voice grew ominous. "They cut the skin off of your flesh, bit by bit, while you watch. They say it's like having your soul torn apart. My great grandfather used to do that to infidels and traitors and once in a while, to disobedient slave girls."

Although she understood few of his words, Fatima had no trouble imagining the Prince making good the terrible threat conveyed by his voice. She knew that there were worse things than being beaten. She had witnessed some of them while a prisoner on Klitzman's island. She would not gamble. She would suck his cock with all of her considerable skill. He could fuck her any which way he pleased. All she knew was that, for the most part, while he was fucking her, he would not be beating her.

Placing his knees on either side of Fatima's head, resting his buttocks on her fiery breasts, he presented his swollen cock to her lips. She parted them readily. Slowly, he plunged inside of her mouth, relishing the hotness inside. Fatima closed her lips around her invader. She licked its tip with her tongue. But it was not the caress of her tongue that the Prince sought. He pressed his cock inexorably deeper and deeper until it breached the entry to her throat.

The girl was well trained at receiving a man's rigid tool down her throat. She let it glide past the entrance and deep within. She expected the Prince to begin to pump his cock inside and out, allowing her, on each backwards thrust, to exchange carbon dioxide for oxygen. But the Prince, once he had reached the extreme of penetration, held himself there. It was not long before the girl began to gag and choke. She tugged madly at her bound wrists wanting desperately to push him off of her. Loud, choking sounds emanated from her throat.

"This is what your mouth is for, you fucking useless

cunt!" the Prince yelled. "Will you swear at me again?"

Frantically, Fatima tried to convey a negative response by a shake of her head.

"You will take what I give you and like it, right, whore?"

Again, Fatima tried furtively to convey her acquiescence.

Seeing that his whore was about to suffocate, the Prince withdrew his rod sufficient for her to regain her breath. He then plunged in again, this time pumping furiously. The French girl gasped for air at each opportunity as the Prince drove himself to his orgasm. His belly slammed against her face again and again as he thrust brutally into her mouth. Finally, she felt him stiffen and heard a long, angry groan. He pumped his hot seed down her throat. She received it gratefully, knowing that her ordeal would soon end. When he had gasped his last, he slowly withdrew his softening tool.

The girl could see that the Prince had exhausted his forces. He stood up from the bed, practically teetering. "Soon, soon," she prayed. "Let him pass out soon!"

He took another long pull from the bottle. When he placed it back on the credenza, it tumbled over, spilling its amber liquid. The Prince either did not notice, or did not care. There was one more thing he had to do. He stumbled over to the cabinet and withdrew a thick, heavy riding crop. He paused between the girl's splayed and uplifted thighs. "Tomorrow, you're going to remember this," he said.

Without further warning, the Prince slammed the riding crop down on the sole of Fatima's foot. Ungagged now, the bound girl howled in pain. She had never felt anything like this brutal insult to the muscles of her foot. The crop came down again on her other foot. She howled again, "Ahhhhhhhhhhhhh! Please stop! Please stop! Please!"

Disregarding the girl's soulful entireties, the Prince slammed he crop again and again on the bottom of her feet. Each time, she jerked her hips and knees and arched her back, unable to endure the pain. She begged him plaintively to stop. The cruel Prince ignored her entreaties, and landed blow after solid blow on the soles of the poor girl's feet. When he stopped, the Prince, sweating and near to swooning in his drunkenness, crept over to the side of the bed. He placed his lips close to Fatima's ear. Tears were streaming down her face, her lips cemented into a fierce grimace. "Tomorrow," he said, whispering, "I'm going to make you stand all day on those feet. You don't know what agony is yet, bitch."

Fatima spent the night hogtied and gagged at the foot of Rashan's bed, her feet throbbing and aching with pain. In the morning, when Ngomo came to collect her, the Prince gave specific orders that she was to remain in his room until further orders. He instructed the slave master that, after she was fed and groomed, she was to spend the day standing, affixed to the chain that ran to the ceiling in the middle of the room. He then left to pursue his pleasures elsewhere.

The day had been a long and agonizing one for the French girl. Her feet were bruised and swollen where she had been beaten the night before by that demon, Rashan. It was exquisite torture to stand on them. She moaned and cried all day. Ngomo gave her some succor from her ordeal by releasing her for short periods and icing down her soles. He knew that he was risking the Prince's wrath, but he could not allow the girl to suffer so. When he reaffixed Fatima to the chain, her pulled her arms taut over her head so that she could rest some of her weight on her wrists.

In the late afternoon, two servants came in carrying a large steel cage. Its bottom was lined with padding. They were followed by the Prince. Fatima was hanging lifelessly at the chain. The pain from her feet absorbed her whole being. The Prince grabbed her by the cheeks and pointed her face at the cage. "Your new home, cunt. I hope you enjoy it."

He nodded to the servants, who released Fatima and dragged her slouched form over to the cage. The Prince ordered her to get in. Morosely, not caring whether she lived or died, the slave girl complied. She was, as the Prince had promised, still gagged, and had been so all day except when Ngomo came in to feed her and give her liquids to drink.

From this day on, Fatima never left the Prince's room. She fucked him listlessly, accepted his insults and violence. She would no longer scream in pain, but merely moaned, a piteous, low guttural moan, when the Prince wantonly beat her.

About ten days after Fatima's ordeal began; she was removed from her cage by Ngomo. She was so far gone that she hardly noticed being carried from the room. She awoke in a bed in a small, strange room. It was plainly decorated, with stark white walls and a small nightstand. Her ankle was chained to the corner of the bed, but otherwise, she was unconfined. A man came

in, gave her a pill, and she lapsed back into uncon-
sciousness.

No one spoke to her, and, although she was not
gagged, she asked no questions. She spent her days
mostly sleeping. Gradually, over a three-day period, her
wounds began to heal, the dark purple bruises to fade.
Fatima was certain that at any moment she would be
dragged back to the Prince's room. Was she being
rested so that she could endure more of his torments?
When she thought of what awaited her outside of her
room, she pulled the sheets over her head and cried.

On the morning of the fourth day, Ngomo came
into to the room. She was finally able to stand without
incapacitating pain and he pulled her to her feet. She
looked up at him, resigned to being returned to her
hellish prison. She stood there listlessly as her hands
were tied behind her back. Ngomo turned her around
to face him. Her eyes met his, forlorn in aspect. Her
lips trembled, her eyes watered. She feared to beg for
mercy from this giant, her master's servant.

Ngomo looked back at Fatima. "No, little one," he
told her, "the Prince, *ille mort*, dead. You never have to
go back there again."

Tears rolled down the French girl's face. She started
to sob. All of the pain and misery of the last two weeks
came pouring out of her. The Prince was dead. God's
justice meted out to him. At the time, the French girl
had no inclination to wonder why or how the Prince
had died. It was a miracle as far she was concerned and
miracles are not questioned. The slave master, whose
iron will ruled the Emir's harem, softly rubbed the
sobbing girl's head, comforting her. As her crying

subsided, the tall, chocolate colored man lifted her chin. He proffered a small leather ball to her mouth. Fatima accepted it meekly.

It was the drinking, you see, that finished the Prince. He had bought himself a brand new Harley Davidson Roadster and was showing it off to his friends. He had been partying all afternoon and did not see the truck approaching. He and another of his dissolute set, who was riding on the back, were literally flattened. There was an investigation, but the truck driver managed to slip from the country. It was rumored that certain of the wealthy merchants and property owners of the Emirate had been sanguine over the prospect of being ruled by the Emir's son. But nothing was ever proved.

The French girl was escorted through the palace in the normal fashion. She was stopped at the end of a hallway and she was surprised when some kind of hooded garment was draped over her. It was a burkha, which covered her body from head to foot. She heard a door open and then felt smooth, cool concrete under her feet. A car door opened and she was hustled in.

Fatima, although relieved and ecstatic over the Prince's death, was apprehensive as to her destination. Had she been sold? Who would be her new master? Would he be cruel and sadistic like the Prince? "But who could be as savage as that man?" she thought. In the end, it was all the same. She was a nameless chattel doomed to a miserable life and an ignominious end.

After a drive of about twenty minutes, Fatima felt the car slow and then turn into a driveway. The car stopped and she was removed from it. She was guided up some short steps and then brought inside to a softly carpeted room. She felt the burkha being removed and she was then led by a chain from her collar down a long hallway. There were many twists and turns, but she finally was brought to a halt. She felt the chain released. Her hands were untied, the hood pulled off of her head, the leather ball removed. Standing before her, dressed in a long, silken robe, her face gleaming with happiness, was the Princess Alliyah.

The French girl was overcome with joy. She had never dreamed that she would see the Princess again. She treasured the memories of their night of bliss together. The Princess beamed at her. "Welcome to my home," she said in French.

The girl's eyes widened with surprise. The Princess spoke French! How it soothed her ears to hear it. She hardly dared to speak herself. The servants who had brought her discreetly left the room. When they had gone, The Princess embraced her.

"Oh, Fatima, if you only knew how my heart has ached for you. How I cried and cried when I learned of the cruel torments that Rashan had inflicted on you. Please, please speak to me. Tell me that you love me too!"

The Princess embraced the stunned but happy slave girl. They hugged each other like old school chums. Fatima's naked body rubbed up against the Princess's. Alliyah began to kiss her face hungrily. Overwhelmed with happiness, the slave girl reciprocated. They were in a large, finely decorated boudoir and there was a large, four posted bed in its center. Alliyah dragged her lover towards it and pulled her down, smothering the slave girl's luscious, hot body with her own.

Shedding her delicate robe, the Princess was naked beneath. She delved into Fatima's mouth with her hot tongue, crushing her lips. Her hand seized the young woman's sex and caressed it. She ran her hand over Fatima's tender belly, across her hip, down her thigh. Abandoning her lips, Alliyah kissed the tips of Fatima's breasts, sucking long and hard on the nipples and bringing a moan to the girl's lips. Fatima's pussy was now moistened and soft. She had thought that she would never feel pleasure from her body ever again, but the Princess's fingers danced tantalizingly on her skin.

Fatima felt the Princess's lips descend from her breasts, over her belly, and to the top of her loins. Blissfully, she looked down at her royal lover. Alliyah looked up, her face a mask of joy.

"I've learned something since we last met, Fatima," she said as she drew the girl's legs apart. She stroked the inside of the thighs delicately. Her hands came to rest astride the slave girl's throbbing mound. Fatima felt hot lips seize her clitoris. The mouth sucked gently on it. Wave after wave of pleasure ran through her. She took the Princess's hair in her hands, caressing the head that lay between her legs.

Alliyah stroked the tender, pink flesh between Fatima's distended and engorged labia with her long tongue. Again and again, she ran its hot surface along the gushing slit. Fatima moaned wildly. As the Princess's mouth again found her point of pleasure, the French girl cried out in ecstasy. She felt her pussy throb and contract. Her mind clouded over, the eager lips and tongue that massaged her rigid clit became the center of her universe. As her orgasm overcame her, she released all of her pain and joy, calling out wildly, "Oh! Oh! Ohhhhhhhhhh!"

Afterwards, the Princess rested her head on Fatima's stomach, her body recumbent between the slave girl's knees. Rubbing her lover's head gently, Fatima dared to speak. "Oh, mistress," she whispered, "I can't tell you how I feel."

The Princess looked up. "You belong to me now Fatima, but it is I who am the slave. Please tell me that you love me too!"

"I do, mistress, I do," Fatima replied. She pulled her mistress's body up close and kissed her. The Princess's mouth accepted her tongue. The two young women remained locked into their embrace, while their tongues expressed their mutual passion and love. After a moment, Fatima broke off the kiss. She looked deeply into her mistress's eyes, searching for reassurance. "How can this be, mistress? Can I really stay here with you?"

"Oh, yes," the Princess told her quickly. "I'm married now. I was married two weeks ago, a few days after the night we made love." The Princess blushed and cast her eyes downward. "That is how I learned the caresses that I just gave you. My husband is a wonderful lover."

"But what will become of me?" the French girl asked, nervously.

The Princess took Fatima's hands in hers. "In my country," she said, "the men rule the world, the women rule the house. You will be called my servant, but you will be my lover and my companion. You will be constantly at my side."

"But your husband?"

"He has agreed. He is a kind and gentle man. I want to share you with him," the Princess answered, her eyes glistening with tears. "I want all of us to be lovers. Will you do that? Please say 'yes'."

Fatima's eyes softened, her hand caressed the Princess's tender, round breast, teasing the pert nipple until the Princess emitted a sigh of incipient lust. The French girl, Fatima, as she now was known, lowered her head to take the Princess's taut, plump nipple into her mouth. She smiled and spoke as she subsumed it, "It is as my mistress commands."

CODA

NOTHING LASTS FOREVER

Alliyah kept her promise to the slave girl, Fatima. That night, she introduced her to her husband's bed and the three of them spent hours in carnal delight. While Alliyah maintained her role as wife and consort to her husband, fourth in line for the throne, managing his household and having his babies, Fatima was permitted to hold sway over the vast gardens that adjoined their estate. Often, Alliyah would come upon her planting new colorful and exuberant delights, only to draw her away to her bedroom where she could drink at the well of her succulent flesh.

In the year following Rashan's death, the health of the Emir declined. Like many a doting and permissive father, he regretted not taking Rashan in hand during his younger years, not schooling him in the duties of those blessed by nobility. Eighteen months after Rashan's death, the Emir passed on, to the sorrow of the people and, of course, his family. Dismayed by the seeming corruption of his male line, the Emir anointed Alliyah's husband as his successor before he died. Fatima reluctantly returned to the Palace, which had been the scene of her former torments.

Alliyah's husband, the Emir, was a graduate of Cambridge University and had been a vocal advocate of the modernization of his country. He was an adherent of a more secularized version of Islam and vowed to move his country out of the dark ages. Slavery, as soon as he consolidated his hold on power, was to be abolished. This was somewhat of a delicate matter since, for many years, slavery had been confined to the female variety and consisted, primarily, of nubile, young women from various Western countries.

Fatima was happy to be reunited with her former slave sisters. Jamilah and Me Ling were still there. To Fatima's dismay, her lover Gelela had been sold to a lesser prince the year before. She begged Alliyah to find her and buy her back, but the Princess was unable to discover any information as to her fate.

Nonetheless, life in the Palace for the slave girls became pleasant and, almost, joyful. Due to the formalities of state and the arcane customs of the country, the slave girls, all but for Fatima, were required to serve the Emir's guests at the various formal and informal dinners necessary to the proper administration of the country, and to the consolidation of political power. The country's male elite expected the service of willing and accomplished sexual slaves at the Emir's gatherings.

It was the Emir's opposition to the building of the American naval base that started the real trouble. As a matter of national pride, the Emir opposed it and the prospective overrun of his country by the immensely powerful commercial interests that would follow. There was a coterie of nobles and wealthy businessmen who deplored the rumors of the prospective banishment of their favorite institution and who coveted the prospect of the river of cash that an American base would produce. But, mainly, to be deprived of the flesh of abjectly serving women was a thing not to be endured.

Ultimately, the combination of strong external interests, the American State Department, and the machinations of an alliance of influential internal conspirators, prompted the coup. The Emir was shot out of hand, as was the dowager Queen. There was a brief, intense firefight between soldiers loyal to the Emir and the rebels, but when word of the death of the Emir spread, the fighting ceased.

The new Emir assumed the property and duties of the old. The bevy of beautiful slaves that had graced the happy Palace was sold off. It would not do to have creatures who had been despoiled by dreams of freedom to be gathered together under the Emir's roof. Fatima, the ill-fated French girl, was among them. Her destination was never revealed to the Princess.

As partial payment to the nefarious organization that had been recruited to surreptitiously supply the rebels with arms to equip their followers, and gold to buy the loyalty of high ranking army officers, the comely and youthful among the wives and daughters of those officials who remained loyal to the Emir were delivered, en mass, to a small island off the coast of west Africa. There they soon found emblazoned on their rear quarters a bright red, two inch high, cursive "*k*".

* * * * * * * * * * * * *

* * * * * * * * * * * * * * *

This is the story of the French girl as told to me by a comely, acquiescent female who called herself Alliyah, and who served me as my body slave for a week in the winter of 2003.

Harry Wiggins

End of Book One